Blind Aphrodite

Blind Aphrodite

Renee Bernard

Writers Club Press
San Jose New York Lincoln Shanghai

Blind Aphrodite

All Rights Reserved © 2000 by Renee Bernard

No part of this book may be reproduced or transmitted in any form or by any means, graphic, electronic, or mechanical, including photocopying, recording, taping, or by any information storage or retrieval system, without the permission in writing from the publisher.

Published by Writers Club Press
an imprint of iUniverse.com, Inc.

For information address:
iUniverse.com, Inc.
620 North 48th Street, Suite 201
Lincoln, NE 68504-3467
www.iuniverse.com

This is a work of fiction. Names, characters, places, and incidents either are the product of the author's imagination or are used fictiously, and any resemblance to actual persons, living or dead, events, or locales is entirely coincidental.

ISBN: 0-595-12069-5

Printed in the United States of America

To Jeannine, who taught me to see
that all miracles are within reach.

ACKNOWLEDGMENTS

I would like to acknowledge all the people who helped to inspire and guide me while writing this book. My special thanks to my editors, Leslie Merriam and Susan Jameson, for keeping me on track. My thanks also to Sara and John Peterson for convincing me that it is never too late. And finally, to Holly Reynolds, for her practical advice and faithful support.

Epigraph

For I weep the world's outcast.
Blind I was, and cannot tell why;
Asleep, for you had given ease of breath;
A fool, while the false years went by.

—Sophocles

Chapter One

1780

A woman's screech of fright from outside made the ancient harbor master push back from his cracked leather books with a smile. His startled young clerk looked up at the shrill sound only to see its apparent cause stride through the doors. The figure gave the illusion of being handsome, a tall, well-formed man in leather leggings and high boots, broad shoulders and a narrow waist accented by the flair and cut of his wool coat. His height was impressive, and he removed a worn black tricorne hat to reveal unpowdered hair the color of burnished gold tied in a casual gather at the nape of his neck. Illusion then met with reality as harsh sunlight touched features that only a demon could possess. The clerk's inkwell overturned unnoticed as he saw the man's face for the first time. 'Used to be a looker—by god," and the thought made his stomach clench at the sight of beauty gone horribly awry. Whereas the right side of his face was a marvel of chiseled lines and hardened male grace, the left side of his face looked as if it had been torn away, and then clumsily put back by a careless hand.

Captain Rutger Grayson heard the inkwell strike the wooden desk's worn surface as clearly as if it were a hammer against an iron spike. Like the trollop's scream in the lane, he considered it another lash he would have preferred to live without. He could count on one hand the number of times he had ventured off his ship in broad daylight during the last few years. The *RavenSong* was his haven as well as his livelihood, and it had only been for the likes of Duncan that he made an unwilling trip from its protective decks. Damn him to hell!

Apparently oblivious to his friend's ill will, Duncan creaked his way around the records table to offer a warm hand. "Tried to send Samson, did ye? For all ye've supposedly left behind them courtier's airs, ye' certainly know how to send dispatches like a royal, ye' ugly dog!"

Rutger took a deep breath and tried not to let Duncan goad him any further. "No offense intended, Duncan, but I didn't see a line of ship's captains outside your door required to make a personal appearance just to make a simple dock fee payment, or to record their cargo."

"For you, I made an exception," Duncan could barely contain his glee now. "Holed up on that ship like Neptune's hermit—you've got to climb off the damn thing once in a while! And what better cause than to see an old friend?"

Duncan's smile was simply too impossible to resist, the old man's pleasure was genuine, if misdirected, and Rutger's own humor answered back with the twisted smile that was his own. The damaged muscles of his left cheek gave the expression the slant of a murderous smirk, but to Duncan it was a great pleasure to behold.

"All right, all right. I'm flattered you would risk me charging in here and breaking your clerk's neck just for the pleasure of my company, you old codger. Now, let me pay my dues and sign the registry and be on my way." Rutger couldn't help but add mischievously, "Tight schedule. More women and children to scare before we set sail."

"It's a talent my friend! I heard poor Sally from here." Duncan led him back to the table, with the dock's registry. "I won't keep ye' from yer precious solitude, Muck. Just sign me books and then have a quick whiskey with an old codger, won't ye?"

Rutger moved to oblige him, taking a worn quill to the pages laid out for him. His nickname, 'Muck', was reserved for a chosen few that knew him well enough to hazard it. Unlike the cries and comments in the streets, it never carried any harm to his heart. Instead it always felt like a simple sign of acceptance and affection, despite its reference to what was apparently left of his face.

"The whiskey at least sounds good," he growled good-naturedly as he signed the ship's register and laid his line fees across the table. "Although, I'd have invited you aboard the *Song* for better, and you'd have saved me getting the evil eye from the fish monger and that bar maid."

"Pshht! Idiots, all of them!" He snarled defensively, "Including that baggage staring from the corner!" He raised his voice and threw a measuring weight towards the corner, as the young man scurried to avoid the missile easily. It seemed Duncan regularly used this method to catch his clerk's attention—without much success by the looks of the dents on the walls. Duncan fished out a jug from underneath a table bowed by a mountain of paper. "Besides, ye'll have grown soft with all that expensive swill. If ye're a sailor, then ye'll drink a man's best brew and mind yer manners."

Rutger accepted the small wooden cup and tossed back what he hoped didn't amount to poison judging from the smell. He managed to keep a straight face, and avoid a coughing fit only by the narrowest margin. At least until Duncan gave him a good-hearted clap on the back for his efforts, and caused him to lose the battle. When the spasms finally subsided, they were both laughing.

"Congratulations, Duncan," Rutger gasped, still recovering, "You've discovered how to make whiskey out of old register books and sea kelp."

"Well, so much for yer fine taste—that's top grade, my friend!" Duncan sputtered; taking another shot just to prove its quality and finding himself doubled over by the burning sensation in his throat.

"I should leave you to your best brew, Duncan," Rutger took his turn patting Duncan gently on the back until his aged friend appeared to have his breathing back under control.

Blind Aphrodite

"Off so soon? You only just walked though the door," the plea's sincerity held him only for an instant.

The light seemed to dim in Rutger's lion-gold eyes, "You refused to accept the line fees from Samson, and brought me all the way into this shack to sign, pay and drink. I have signed, paid and had a drink. We leave in two days, and there is a great deal of work to be done before then. What else would you like me to do for your amusement? Sing arias in the square, dance a jig to make children cry or should I just wait until its dark before I creep back to the *RavenSong*?" Bitterness made his words harsher than Rutger had ever intended them, his frustration shaking mirth from his reach.

Duncan's chin came up in reaction, his smile fading fast. "Fine! Head back to your badger hole, and good riddance. But mind me, Muck, you can't hide from the world forever. You can sail along its edges and lie to yourself to say that 'along it' is the same as 'in it', but it's a lie all the same. So forgive an old man for trying to pry you out from under your rock into the sunlight."

Rutger turned on his heels without another word, fury carrying him along the cobbled streets and back towards his beloved ship. Duncan's speech rang in his ears, almost drowning out the sporadic gasps and quick cries of the people he passed on the crowded street. Almost. Rutger found himself renewing his vow to keep to the shadows and to avoid at all costs well-meaning old men.

Chapter Two

Rutger paused at the foot of the gangplank, letting his eyes roam over the lines of the *RavenSong*. Pride filled his heart to see her polished rails and new rigging, even while his critical eyes took note of brass lanterns in need of buffing, and a dozen other minor projects. Despite his ire at the forced errand, he enjoyed the rare viewpoint of standing dockside in the sunlight to survey his 'floating kingdom'. He had made sure that the *RavenSong* was one of the trimmest vessels to sea, her comforts only balanced by the demands of economy and trade. Even now, she looked to him as if she were straining at the ropes that held her to land, anxious to return to sea to show off for him.

"You look like a man in love, Captain," Samson's hail brought Rutger out of his reverie with a smile.

"And what's not to love?" he answered his first mate, making his way easily up the swaying gangplank. "She's the most faithful and beautiful creature to part waves. She does as I ask her, and has yet to argue or complain."

"I won't bother to ask you how it was," Samson's brow furrowed with guilt, still stung by old Duncan's stubborn game to draw Muck off the ship. Samson felt a certain measure of protectiveness when it came to his friend, a sentiment shared by the rest of the crew. They viewed their captain like a golden jungle cat, scarred and mangled, but still a powerful hunter and a great soul. In port, they acted as his shield. At sea, they were more like family. Rutger was generous with the profits, and quick to act in

Blind Aphrodite

his crew's best interests. His even-handed style of leadership made them each feel like a partner in their ventures, although each man on the *Song* had no illusions as to whose voice carried real power. Rutger welcomed input, but never allowed disrespect or open dissension. Rutger owned the *RavenSong* outright, and if he chose to land a sailor with a small severance of coins and his belongings to preserve harmony aboard ship, he did so.

"Don't trouble yourself, Samson," Rutger replied, answering his friend's expression of concern, "I should be thankful that he meant well, at least. I am back, safe and sound, aboard the Song, and Duncan's mischief is behind us."

Samson nodded in gratitude and Rutger turned to head down the companionway to his private quarters, settling in to lose himself in mundane paperwork. Time slipped away quickly as he navigated endless lists and ledger lines, preparing drafts for deposit and last minute supply orders. He found peace and felt his own center of balance recovering behind a quiet wall of numbers and the muffled sounds of the ship's work around him.

Rutger leaned back in his chair, and felt the calming magic of the *RavenSong* pour over him. 'Safe and sound', he thought even as an echo of Duncan's chiding came back to him. 'Neptune's hermit, indeed.' But the words rang with a dark truth as he looked about his comfortable sanctuary. Mahogany and rosewood gleamed in the slant of afternoon sun that came through thick glass panes, and open shutters. A master craftsman and apprentices had carved all the beams and columns several years before. The artists' labors giving the illusion of delicate vines and exotic flowers that bloomed year-round in startling honeyed hues. At the time, Rutger had been whole, and had commissioned the extravagance with a mind towards softening a naturally masculine environment for the eventual arrival of a wife or mistress for long voyages. Even at his most rakish, he had held no aspirations to permanent bachelorhood. He had simply been biding his time for the right woman to end his appetite for the chase.

Unfortunately, the chase had ended in a way he had never anticipated, and the wooden garden he had created out of a rogue's fantasy, had instead become another reminder of the green paths he would never walk, and the woman who would never arrive.

Even so, the room's comforts gave him pleasure, and he had spent most of his efforts in adding to its welcome spirit, ignoring painful memories and seeking to block out any thoughts of the future he had lost. Self-pity was a mental state he avoided at all costs, and prided himself on his self-reliance and independence. Rutger told himself it was only his pride that had been stung in the narrow port streets, and nothing more dire. It was Duncan's thoughtlessness that troubled him, and certainly not the buxom creature that had begun to cry out her sweetest invitation, only to scream and then spit after him as his shadow passed.

"If I'm a hermit, it is simply the choice of a rational man to avoid the idiots of the world," he told himself firmly, adding with a twisted smile, "And their idiot daughters." Rutger forced his attentions back to a list he had begun for new volumes for the ship's library, when the sound of Samson's familiar rap came at the door. "Come in, Samson," he hailed quickly.

"Capt. Grayson," Samson's tone and formal greeting warbled to catch Rutger's complete attention. "Two ladies have come aboard and are asking to see you."

Rutger felt his face go numb and wondered if his jaw had fallen open in shock. The use of the word 'ladies' was paralyzing. He had never heard Samson use the term before when describing creatures of the opposite sex. Samson tended toward cruder descriptions, at least when Rutger had overheard him talking to the other men about his 'offshore entertainments'. Even respectable women outside of Samson's realm were generally described by him as 'churched fillies', and so Rutger was sure it was shock alone that caused his reaction. As if watching from a distance, he heard himself answer, "Show them in, Mr. Guilford."

Blind Aphrodite

The moment unfurled like something in a nightmare, as Rutger realized that the door to his sanctuary was about to fall. He tried to take back the directive, but Samson was gone in a flash of obedience and he could only sit and wait for the inevitable scene and horrified reactions from these two mysterious 'ladies' when they saw his face. In his panic, he marveled at the strange stillness of his thoughts where he expected a whirlwind. He only prayed that this sense of disconnection would sustain him until his intruders were long gone.

At Samson's knock, the dreamlike fugue vanished and Rutger felt the afternoon's bruises afresh in anticipation of this next uninvited bout. Samson sheepishly peeped his head in face flushed, and then opened the door to allow their guests to pass into the room. Any false hopes that this was only a jest evaporated in two clouds of colored silk and feminine finery.

Astonishment replaced every other emotion for Rutger, as the most beautiful woman he had ever seen entered the room on the arm of her companion and guardian. Even as he registered the expression of distaste on the second woman's face apparently from her impressions of Samson's major domo skills, and then her gasp of horror, he felt his entire being center on the classic beauty at her side. The young woman's rich coloring shone against her friend's more fashionable pale pastels and Rutger wondered how it could be possible to match this moment for sheer impact. The ebony silk of her curls set off ivory skin and lush features, but her eyes captured him instantly in their blue-green depths, clear and unwavering.

His breath caught in his chest as a smile came naturally to her face to enhance the sweet bow of her lips, and without an instant's hesitation, she stepped forward in a rustle of sapphire-hued silk to offer a gloved hand. Years of pain fell away at the gesture, and Rutger marveled at the appearance of Aphrodite herself in his cabin and the priceless gift of acceptance.

"Captain Grayson, I presume?" her voice was sensuously low, her tone cultured and even.

She had never flinched, and Rutger made his way around the table to be able to take the hand she offered in greeting. He wanted to crow at the simple triumph of looking into a woman's eyes again and seeing only—cold reality swept triumph from his reach. The gloved hand that she extended had been misdirected only an inch or two, but she made no correction as he shifted position. The truth revealed in her gesture struck him with ferocity as all the clues fell into place—her open gaze and easy smile, her companion's guiding arm and the fashionably slim ivory handled bamboo walking stick elegantly looped over her wrist. The rush of his emotions made him feel physically ill; especially when he realized that what he felt most strongly was a sense of relief.

Aphrodite was blind.

"Captain Grayson?" Claire forced herself to keep her hand extended, fearing that if she allowed nerves to get the better of her at this point; she would never be able to accomplish her true mission. Many people were uncomfortable at her blindness, and so Claire attributed his hesitation to take her hand to this.

"At your service, Miss—?" a strong hand enveloped hers, his rich voice matching his touch in warmth as he waited for someone to supply an introduction.

Claire's companion, Miss Olivia Kent recovered somewhat at the question, and although still a shade paler than usual, straightened her shoulders to intervene for protocol's sake. "Capt. Grayson, may I present Miss Claire Aylesbury, sister to Lord Edward Aylesbury, the fourth Earl of Clarence and the Duke of Banbury's only niece. I am her companion, Miss Kent."

Rutger raised an eyebrow at the lofty introduction and would have made a cutting comment to Miss Kent about pedigreed ladies and their companions when he caught the color in Miss Aylesbury's cheeks as she looked away from him for the first time—in embarrassment.

Blind Aphrodite

"I am at your service, Miss Aylesbury," Rutger felt old instincts engage as he bowed over the slender fingers in his own and then reluctantly released them, rewarded as Claire's eyes lifted to flash their colors toward his. "And to what do I owe this unexpected honor?"

"Well—" Claire began only to find herself cut off by her impatient companion.

"To hysteria, Captain!" Olivia's color seemed to be returning quickly as she reassessed their host. "I am still in shock that Miss Aylesbury insisted on such an interview, at risk to our reputations, and now to find ourselves in your—" her eyes darted to the large four poster bed in the room's far corner, "your—quarters is completely unaccept—"

"Thank you, Olivia," Claire's voice was quiet but firm, and seemed to stun a now sputtering Miss Kent into silence. "Perhaps Mr. Guilford would be kind enough to provide you with a tour of the ship while I have a moment with Captain Grayson. Alone." She turned to Rutger and he picked up her unspoken cue for support instantly.

"Of course," he chimed in, striving to keep a straight face at the comic scene that seemed to be unfolding in front of him, "Mr. Guilford!"

Samson, as Rutger had guessed, had not gone far, but had been eavesdropping just outside the door. Even as Miss Kent caught her breath to begin to express her indignation at this abrupt dismissal, Samson had her by the arm and began to lead the protesting creature out of the room.

"This is highly improper! I cannot believe you realize—" Olivia's tone was strident, and Claire flinched but held her ground. Samson gave an ungentlemanly tug to start the tour and closed the door behind them both with the words, "Now, as ships go, the *RavenSong* is one of the finest for her crew and their pride in her fast—."

"Oh my!" Claire felt as if all the air had suddenly been pulled from her lungs at the sound of the door closing. She felt overwhelmed at her circumstances, and wondered at her own audacity to insist on being alone with Capt. Grayson. Her heart hammered in her chest with nerves, and she prayed that her fear didn't appear openly on her face.

"Please, why don't you take a seat, Miss Aylesbury, and make yourself more comfortable," his voice was genial, and as she nodded agreement, she felt his hand guide her easily to a chair. Expecting some simple wooden bench, Claire was surprised to feel the padded seat and soft leather covered arms and curved chair back. It was a small detail that she attributed to a facet of Capt. Grayson's character. His voice was measured and his accent betrayed his good breeding and education, not what Claire had expected of a 'rough seaman' from Olivia's dire warnings.

She decided that she must seize this moment of opportunity, or be lost forever, and with one more deep breath, plunged ahead. "Thank you for your understanding, Capt. Grayson. I will try to be brief. The harbormaster, Mr. Duncan Cliff, pointed me in your direction. I was looking for someone well-traveled, who could perhaps give me some advice." She paused, as if not sure how to go on.

"Ah! Duncan! That explains a great deal," he interjected, bitter amusement coloring his words and causing a small frown to cross her features before Claire recovered to continue.

"It's my brother, Edward." Claire tried to keep her voice level, "He was always a bit of a free spirit, and he had decided to see the world before finally settling down and returning to England to manage the estate. I supported his decision whole-heartedly, and must confess I felt as if through his letters and stories, I was the one who had been voyaging these last three years. But now I've received no word from him for over five months. I'm afraid something terrible has happened."

"Five months is quite a length of time," Rutger paused, unsure of a way to allay her fears.

"Edward is alive, Captain," her voice rang with conviction. "He is more than just a brother to me. He is my twin soul. I know it sounds strange,

Blind Aphrodite

but if he were dead, I would simply know it. We share a bond that is almost impossible to describe. We were always together—getting into adventures, riding and hunting. When I broke my arm in a riding accident, Edward was away at university, but he knew something was wrong and came home instantly. Can you imagine it? Without a word from anyone, he stood up in the middle of a lecture and simply walked out to hire a coach home." A shadow seemed to pass over her eyes, "Five minutes or five months, he is in trouble and he needs me."

"How can I help?" he asked simply, and Claire felt as if a great weight had been lifted from her shoulders.

"Edward's last letter didn't say where he was. His letters are so detailed, I am convinced that someone more seasoned by travel might actually recognize the location just from his descriptions. I've had it read to me a hundred times, but my own knowledge is so limited. If I knew where he had been last, I would at least know where to start an inquiry. Olivia is convinced that I am obsessed. My uncle tells me he has had no word, and is making every effort, but he has been very ill of late. Time is running out. How can I just sit idly by?" Claire knew she was babbling, and stopped herself only with the greatest of efforts. "Please, Capt. Grayson, can you look at this letter and study it to let me know what you can discern?" Nervous hands reached inside her reticule and held the letter out to him across the surface of his work desk.

Rutger had prepared himself to hear a task suited to Hercules from the seriousness in her tone and the ominous start to her story. He tried to keep the relief out of his voice, "It seems a simple favor, Miss Aylesbury. I can, at the very least, read it to see if something leaps from the page to give you a clue as to his last whereabouts." He took the letter, carefully unfolding its well-worn pages, the ink showing clear evidence of tears from a heart-broken sister's blind eyes. Just as he considered telling her that perhaps it would take time to go over each landmark and consider possible matches—he looked up to wonder if this was just another cruel joke of Duncan's making.

"Are you sure this is his last letter?" his voice sounded wary, even to his own ears.

"Of course! I carry it with me always," Claire's temper flared at the insinuation that she would go to all this trouble over the wrong piece of paper.

The fiery green storm that leapt into her eyes made his heart somersault in the cage of his chest, and Rutger wondered if it were possible to have imagined her capable of any secrets, "I don't mean to offend you, Miss Aylesbury. The date on the letter is as you say, five months old, but the origin is clearly stated underneath it. Savannah, a port in the American colonies still occupied by our forces I believe. I see no great mystery for resolution. Are you sure you—?"

His words were cut off by the stricken look on her face, followed by one of dawning horror at his revelation. Rutger could see the fear racing through her slim frame, as if he had just calmly announced that he was going to kill her. "Are you all right? Shall I call your companion?"

"No!" Claire came shakily to her feet, sure that whatever measure of control remained to her would not be enough to withstand Olivia's sharp tongue in this instant. "I mean," she took a shallow breath to try to mask her panic, "Please give me back my letter."

Rutger folded her precious paper, and held it back across the table, "Here you are, Miss Aylesbury." He placed it into her shaking hand, feeling completely helpless at this strange turn in their interview.

"I've already taken up too much of your time, Captain Grayson. Thank you for your assistance." She put the letter back into her purse and shifted to stand away from the chair, her walking stick sliding to her hand as a subtle guide. Claire held herself stiffly, waiting only for him to summon Mr. Guilford back with Olivia so that she could be away from this truth she didn't want to hear.

Blind Aphrodite

"Please wait," he spoke while closing the space between them, "Clearly there is more going on here, and while I realize that I am a complete stranger to you and your brother, I cannot help but to feel concerned. Tell me what is happening."

The sincerity in his voice reached through the haze of her panic, and Claire was amazed to discover that she trusted this complete stranger. She detected no pity in the even timbre of his voice. He stood next to her row, the clean strong scent of the ocean mixed with soap and sandalwood, his presence one of size and strength. She felt a strange urge to cry on his shoulder and tell him everything—just to hear his deep, melodious voice whisper foolish words of comfort. 'A complete stranger, but I hadn't realized until this moment that there wasn't anyone else I could trust,' an inner voice mourned.

Just as she wavered to decide to confide in him, the sound of quick footsteps and Olivia's unmistakable complaints reached her ears. Claire lowered her voice, desperation coloring each word, "Please don't mention the letter to her, I beg you!"

As the door to his cabin burst open, Rutger instinctively took a step away from Claire, purposefully looking calm in the face of Olivia's chaotic entrance with a panting and relieved Samson in tow.

Claire addressed Rutger again, her tone louder and serious, making him marvel at the lightening speed of the change in her. "What a shame you hadn't heard of any distant shipwrecks or storms that may have prevented Edward's return! With all your experience and connections, I was sure that you may have provided us with an important clue." She extended her hand again, causing his own mechanical response to take it briefly.

Rutger admired her strength, and played along with the farewell, noting the narrowed eyes and suspicious looks of her guardian.

"I am so sorry I was no great help," Rutger also nodded politely to Olivia, who stepped in to reclaim her charge as she captured Claire's free hand.

"Ah! Olivia," Claire lamented, "Your timing is perfect, as you can see, you were right all along. It seems I have been overly stubborn." Her eyes filled with tears, and she was unable to go on.

"Well, don't be too hard on yourself, dearest," Olivia soothed, "Edward was dear to you, as he was to us all, and a loss like that is never easy to accept." She turned to the Captain, eyes bright as a hawk, "I apologize for this bizarre intrusion into your working day, Captain Grayson. As you can see, Miss Aylesbury is inclined to let her grieving imagination have full rein."

Rutger decided there was very little he liked about Miss Olivia Kent, but even less he could do about it at this moment. "Yes, of course. I am sorry to hear of your loss, Miss Aylesbury. I hope you will find your spirit much restored soon." The words were sincere as he watched Claire led meekly away—his own spirit now much unsettled by the mysterious disappearance of her brother and the twists of fate that brought her onto the *RavenSong*.

* * *

"Well, you've got Duncan to thank for that little fiasco!" Samson's indignation was unmistakable. "What the hell was that all about? Ladies! On this ship! Next thing you know, he'll have one of their little societies drop over for tea, for bleedin—"

"Samson, please." Rutger cut him off, turning to face the windows. "I think I can already guess where the rest of that speech is going, so why not spare me?"

"Well, I don't know about the one you had your talk with, but that hellcat you had me baby-sit was a nightmare in crinolines, I'm telling you!" Rutger glanced over his shoulder to catch the smile on Samson's face that belied his words. They had been friends long enough for Rutger to be aware that his first mate had always enjoyed women with a

Blind Aphrodite

streak of hellcat in them. Just as Rutger considered teasing Samson about his latest paramour, Samson continued, "My imagination, Muck, or was that pretty thing blind?"

The question caught him off guard, and Rutger felt a lump form in this throat. The image of her standing in his cabin leapt back into his mind's eye—so beautiful, and brave, a vision in sapphire-blue silk with clear blue-green eyes the color of the sea. A woman that seemed to look straight into his heart, Miss Aylesbury had used no artifice, or coy games, showing only grace in the face of adversity. She hadn't been afraid of him, of course. Being blind had certainly made that an easy feat, but it still didn't stop her from slipping right through his defenses. Worse still, she made him realize how long it had been since a woman had spoken to him as if he was a human being. At least, a woman he hadn't paid in a moment of weakness to pretend he was whole. How many years had it been since he had been able to walk the streets without feeling exposed and ashamed? How much time had passed to allow him to forget what it was to have the attention of every woman in the room, knowing the power to seduce even the most 'reluctant' beauty was his to command? Ballrooms and salons had been a sensual playground, and he had enjoyed the endless welcome that they afforded a young buccaneer aristocrat. It had seemed like centuries had passed; at least until Miss Claire Aylesbury extended one slender gloved hand at the wreck that remained of Captain Rutger Grayson. Now the past felt close enough to touch, and the loss was too great to comprehend.

"Captain? Where'd you go?" Samson ventured hesitantly; aware of the turn the day had taken for his friend. *No women aboard the RavenSong,* Samson reminded himself, *and that rule don't have a damn thing to do with sea-going superstitions. Rakes him over the coals every time we bump into their kind, and there's no gain in it.* "Never mind, sir. We'll not see the likes of them again, and there's business to be seen to."

- 16 -

"You're right. Send Mallory to the post with these, and let me know when the final stores are aboard." Rutger was grateful to return to the refuge of his desk, as Samson jumped to do his bidding. But as the door closed behind him, Rutger ran worried hands through his long hair. "Whoever she is, she's in real trouble—and I'm sure there's not a damn thing I can do about it." The words were hollow in his ears. There probably was something he could do, but Rutger felt his own fear uncoil to hold him in place.

Chapter Three

∞

The carriage ride back to the townhouse was endless for Claire. She kept her eyes down, feeling confined and defeated. Olivia had wasted no time initiating a lecture on proper behavior and the priceless value of a woman's reputation, while managing to weave in a reprise on foolish hopes, the requirements of the real world and the wishes of Claire's uncle. Claire let the words flow past her like brackish water, steeling herself to pay as little attention as possible. Inside she felt as if she might drown in the turmoil of her own thoughts.

Betrayed. Olivia had read the letter to her dozens of times, even commiserating with her on how strange it was that it should not bear a return address or marking of any kind. She reeled with nausea as she recalled being comforted in Olivia's arms, and how she had considered Olivia an ally and protector. How stupid she felt! Olivia had lied all along, and under the guise of practical advice, had been pushing her to accept Edward's death and move on by accepting Lord Forthglade's proposal of marriage.

It was the path she had been hoping never to take. If only Edward would return, then everything could be balanced again. He would protect her and take over the estates as planned. Edward had never forced her to do anything she didn't want to do—he had had more trouble keeping her from doing the things she wanted. If only—

His disappearance seemed even more ominous now, his last letter from a colonial port with war ever present. Why would Olivia lie about the letter's contents? What would she have to gain? Did she have real news about Edward that she was keeping to herself? Did it have anything to do with Lord Forthglade's sudden proposal, or her uncle's prolonged illness? Perhaps Olivia was correct about her over-active imagination, but the danger seemed all too real. She had never felt more blind than she did at this moment, unsure of her own future. Everything seemed to hinge on Edward, either by his heroic and miraculous return, or by discovering the truth of his fate.

"Have you heard a single word I've said, dearest?" Olivia finally managed to break through her wall of misery and panic. "I'm being a tyrant, aren't I? I'm sorry, I suppose it's just this strange errand, and that horrid Mr. Guilford! What a mannerless oaf! I can only imagine what an undignified conversation you must have had with that—"

"Please, Olivia," Claire felt off-balance at Olivia's apparently genuine apology, "I'm the one who is sorry. It has been a disappointing day." The words caught in her throat and she kept her face to the window, while Olivia gave her hand a sympathetic squeeze. The gesture only caused her eyes to fill with tears. Olivia had been her companion since Claire had been fourteen. Only six years older than her charge, Claire had practically worshipped Olivia as the older sister she had never had. Olivia had been so kind and caring, so quick to laugh. When Edward departed on his adventures, Claire had seen him off bravely with Olivia at her side. That same year she had been presented by her uncle as a debutante into formal society, with Olivia acting as chaperone and guardian. It was then that things had begun to change. Olivia had transformed ever so slowly into a solemn mistress, and taken over more and more authority in the household.

When Claire lost her sight, she had depended entirely on Olivia and made a fateful choice not to summon Edward. They had reasoned together that since there was nothing that Edward could do, it would be cruel to end his only chance at freedom before duty confined him to

Blind Aphrodite

hearth and home. It was Olivia who insisted that she continued at least a minimal social schedule, relearning the feminine graces despite her blindness. It was Olivia who had practiced and drilled with Claire endlessly so that she could walk with proper confidence, manage a household staff, dance a simple pattern and serve tea.

She had lived vicariously through Edward's letters, paying little attention to Olivia's firm hand as it guided her through her days of waiting for her brother's return. Now, she wondered at how much independence had slipped soundlessly through her fingers. 'How could I not have noticed the cage until now?' she asked herself silently.

The carriage pulled to a stop, and she recognized the steps of dear old Thomas, their footman. Olivia alighted first, so that she could assist Claire into the house. Claire felt her heart sink, as even the echoes of the familiar hall seemed cold and oppressive. "How is my uncle today, Thomas?"

"Not a good day, miss. He has already retired for the evening and advised us no visits today."

"What a shame!" Olivia's voice was all sympathy and disappointment.

Claire felt the last of her control begin to break, "I think I will just go to my rooms to consider your advice."

"That sounds like a good idea," Olivia said warmly, taking her arm and leading Claire up the stairs. "Despite all my ranting, I am still hopeful that you will suddenly take a practical turn on your own, dearest, without my endless prodding."

"I apologize for being such a burden to you." The words caught in Claire's throat, and the tears that flowed were hot with rage.

Olivia saw only tears of repentance for the day's events and clucked like a mother hen as she helped a now cooperative Claire to bed. She ordered tea, and even offered to brush out Claire's wild curls to soothe her. Without waiting for a response she sat next to Claire and began to pull an ornate silver hairbrush through the soft ebony mass. "There now, isn't that better?" Unseen, Olivia frowned at the waves of dark silk that came to life with each pass of her hand. "Shame the fever dulled its luster," she sighed, ignoring the shine of the candlelight against its ebony strands, rivaling the gleam of the silver. "Perhaps, we should try the powder to hide it."

Finally, Olivia abandoned her ministrations, and decided to leave Claire to her tears of disappointment. As she left, she turned back to look at Claire nestled unhappily in the midst of the room's opulence. She was unable to resist one last push. "You are never a burden to me, dearest. But you may have to consider the burden of worry your uncle carries wanting to ensure that you're cared for if something should happen to him. He would prefer to see you happily wed. You are lucky that your circumstances allow for an advantageous match. A blind woman less provided for and unable to care for herself would be left for institutional care or turned out into the streets."

As the door latched close, Claire felt the weight of the day's revelations settle onto her shoulders. Olivia's parting shot had hit its mark. 'Even a blind lamb could sense the path to slaughter ahead of it,' she shivered as if a cold hand had touched her face. It was to be the match to Lord Forthglade, or she would face a darker future. She would be corralled into it, by her grief for Edward, her guilt and concern for Uncle Trevor and her own fears of being blind and alone.

Unable to lie still, she paced the room unconsciously counting her steps and touching the familiar landmarks that mapped her sanctuary. If only she could stay safely within these walls, it was so much easier to hide from the world outside. The pain was still pressing against her heart, and she felt as if the real truth were still lurking, too horrible to face, but far too menacing to be ignored.

* * *

Blind Aphrodite

Olivia made her way to her own more modest accommodations on the floor above. No spacious chamber of white and gold awaited her, and Olivia ignored the room's simple elegance. She dismissed what she considered cheap brocade and lower quality furnishings. 'All this will change soon enough,' she smiled to herself.

The thing was practically accomplished, and she hugged herself with pleasure at the thought of finally achieving her rightful place. Her parting words to sad little Claire were telling. She knew all too well the heartache of a woman less provided for. Her family lines were still pure enough and near enough to aristocracy for her to truly appreciate the life denied her by sheer mischance. Inept financial management and the consuming habits of her ancestors had ultimately bankrupted the family coffers, leaving each descendant the legacy of a proud name and pauper's pocket. Without a dowry, she had faced the bleak future of a poor spinster and respectable governess.

Providence itself had intervened when she secured her position as companion for Duke Banbury's darling pet niece while Claire's brother, Edward, completed his studies. Their parents had died several years before, and their uncle was sure that Claire would benefit from a female friend and confidante as she neared her debut. At one point in time, she had considered Edward a means to an end, but he had proved to be entirely too devoted to his sister to pay much attention to her advances. In retrospect, she considered this a great blessing, since he was a most unmanageable young man. Claire had proven to be the easier choice, her handicap robbing her of her self-confidence, or at least making her more susceptible to 'good advice'. Easier still had been convincing the failing Duke of his precious niece's fragility and the need for a match to a suitable man.

But Claire wasn't a complete fool, and today's field trip had been a harrowing experience for Olivia. For weeks, Claire had been insistent that Edward must still be alive. Despite mounting proof to the contrary with his prolonged silence, she had proven to be completely intractable. The idea of visiting the docks had taken root several days ago, and Claire had told Olivia that she intended to show the letter to an expert to see what they thought of Edward's whereabouts. Olivia had convinced her that the letter was too valuable to hand over to a stranger—or worse, to lose on some ridiculous and dangerous outing. Claire had finally admitted that since she had the letter memorized, she could just recite the key passages for some dusty old admiral to laugh at before they returned prudently home. It was that concession alone that had allowed the trip to proceed, and Olivia had still quizzed her in the carriage as they set out to ensure that Claire hadn't brought the condemning scrap of paper with her.

What could have been the undoing of Olivia's larger plan, had instead seemed to be a guarantee of her victory. Claire had so convinced herself that someone with intimate knowledge of the seas would be able to tell her Edward's last location, that her disappointment now made her more vulnerable than ever. It was clear that whatever had passed between Claire and her Captain while she was banished from the cabin, it had not offered any consolation to Claire.

The smile on her attractive features twisted into something sardonic as she remembered her first reaction to the sea captain. One cripple had unknowingly sought out another. As angry as she had been to be shunted from the room, a part of her had been glad to escape the sight of his half-destroyed face. It would have been better for him if his entire face were torn and scarred, but it seemed worse to have male perfection on one side turn into the devil himself on the other. They made a charming pair, the blind girl and the monster.

She surveyed her reflection in the mirror by her dressing stand, and inventoried the woman staring back. Still beautiful, the pale yellow of her gown was the perfect foil for her soft coloring, and made her seem very fresh and unspoiled. Despite her golden hair and stark blue eyes, Olivia

Blind Aphrodite

decided that she had very little of the 'porcelain doll' look. Her figure was striking and now at twenty-eight, she would never be mistaken for a dew-eyed innocent. She had taken great pains to try to hide her own voluptuous nature, but recent months had taught her of its power unleashed. Now, even the dark smile pleased her, since it made the woman in the mirror look cruel and untouchable.

She yanked the bell pull to call for a hot bath, and began to hum as she unwound her great long braid for brushing. For tomorrow was Thursday, and she had a dangerous assignation of her own to keep.

Chapter Four

Claire concentrated to make her trembling fingers finish the last of the small hooks at the back of her dress, trying not to hear the chime of the clock over the mantel. Smoothing out the simple skirt, she forced herself to sit in what she hoped was a casual pose at her dressing table. Heart pounding, Claire wondered if by some horrible twist she had lost track of the days, when Olivia's efficient knock and quick entrance laid her fears to rest.

"Oh! You are certainly up very early this morning, dearest!" Olivia's surprise to see Claire fully dressed and waiting was apparent.

Claire answered easily, "I just couldn't sleep and decided that it was just better to rise early and get on with the day."

"You should have woken me," Olivia admonished, eyes studying Claire carefully for any tell-tale changes in color, "I would have helped you dress."

Claire laughed, "You deserve your rest more than anyone! After all that you do for me and for Uncle Trevor, it seemed a small thing to allow you to sleep a while longer." She stood to gather her cane and reticule, trying to keep her movements unhurried.

Olivia's defenses relaxed, "How considerate of you!" She came to take Claire's arm, "Shall we make an early start of it then? Monsieur Joubert should offer a great selection for his first customers of the day."

Olivia chattered happily, as usual looking forward to their weekly outing to the florist. She had always insisted that the house have fresh flowers

Blind Aphrodite

when they were in town, and more importantly, that Claire should master the feminine art of flower arrangement. Olivia had been pleased to find something that Claire could do by touch and smell alone, at least something that passed for a more genteel talent.

For once, Claire was grateful for Olivia's self-involvement, and tried desperately to keep a calm and interested expression on her face. Their trips to the florist had been extremely regimented, and Claire silently prayed that her own disruption to the normal routine wouldn't cause any additional changes. She was relieved to find that, as usual, upon arrival at the shop, Olivia tasked her with sorting through the main room's selection for possibilities, while she selected containers and sorted through the flowers in the back storerooms and greenhouse.

Claire waited, her heart pounding until she was sure that Olivia had gone into the back of the store. With a white-knuckle grip on the ivory handle of her walking stick, she deliberately counted to thirty to be sure, while checking to make sure that her reticule was still firmly tied to her wrist. At thirty, she turned towards the open shop door and stepped out into the early morning light. It had been an easy trip of only ten steps, but Claire felt the enormity of her decision weighing upon her. All her own doubts assaulted her, and the plan that had seemed brilliant and desperate in the middle of the night, now felt foolish. She steeled herself to find the traces of courage she had managed earlier, only to discover sheer panic. Before the fear became paralyzing, she forced herself to walk and count the steps to the corner, moving as quickly as she could towards their own carriage and hired servants. Thomas spotted her first, and came forward to help her up into the carriage.

"Nothing today, miss?" Thomas offered.

"Not at all, Thomas," Claire tried out her most confident smile, "The selection smells lovely and Miss Kent seems very pleased. It's just that I have left my wrap at the townhouse, and we are going to do some additional shopping after we've chosen our arrangements. Can you drive home and get it quickly?"

"Won't that leave you stranded, Miss Claire?" Thomas seemed reluctant.

"Oh, no! I assure you we are enjoying ourselves immensely with so much to choose from. Besides, it is a quick turn back to the house. You'll be back long before we've finished here, and then we'll be ready to visit the dressmakers." Her voice sounded overly bright in her ears, but she kept her gaze steady and pleaded silently for his quick compliance.

Her pleas were answered. "As you say, Miss. We won't be but thirty minutes. Can I escort you back to the shop?"

She waved away his offer, "Thomas, I am perfectly capable of walking ten feet. Honestly!" She didn't give him a chance to protest further, but turned to head back towards the shop door, satisfied to hear Thomas' steps and the sound of the carriage pulling away. She slowed and then turned from the door, and used her cane as a guide to make her way as far down the street as she dared. Only a hundred feet, and Claire stepped to the curb to raise her hand for a hackneyed coach, as she'd seen her uncle do years before. She felt the blood rush to her cheeks in embarrassment—convinced that she must look like a very foolish statue with one hand pointlessly raised. Just as her hand wavered with her thoughts, and she felt the last remnant of momentum and courage start to dissipate, an old man's voice came at her elbow.

"Do you need a carriage, mistress?" her unknown angel offered.

"Yes, thank you, that would be most kind." Relief threatened to make her knees turn to liquid.

"I'll hail Old Jim for you, miss." She felt him step off the curb, followed by the shrillest whistle as he made quick work of catching Jim's attention. Claire fished out a coin from her purse and thanked him again as he helped her into the carriage. She told the driver where to take her and then quickly pulled the shades for privacy, as every nerve began straining for the

Blind Aphrodite

first sounds of alarm. She waited to hear Olivia's screams, or for someone to yell, "Stop that carriage!" but no one seemed to have taken any notice as the carriage pulled briskly into the busy street.

Claire tried to calculate how long it had taken her to leave the shop, dismiss Thomas and to hire a carriage, but her nerves were too frayed for an accurate estimation. Only a minute or two, she told herself, and it would be at least ten or fifteen minutes before Olivia discovered her missing. *A few minutes to look for me nearby and then she'll hopefully see the carriage gone and assume that I returned home. If the fates are kind, she'll head home first, before branching out the search.* The docks had seemed an obvious destination in light of yesterday's events, and Claire knew that her window of opportunity was extremely brief.

If Captain Grayson wasn't aboard, or if his concern yesterday had only been a polite gesture—if he refused to help, or was unwilling to become involved, her escape would end there.

To calm herself, she tried to reconstruct Edward's face and recall the sound of his voice. Edward would have been brave and laughed at all this foolishness. Edward would never cower in a shaded carriage clinging to the straps like a drowning man. Calm overcame her as she felt his invisible presence steadying her in the carriage. Her courage returned and she took a deep breath, releasing the hand strap and sitting back on the cushions. Oddly, Edward's face wavered, and in her head, she heard another voice— deeper than her brother's familiar tones, but still comforting. Suddenly, it was Capt. Grayson she considered, imagining a face to match his measured, practical manner of speech. He was tall, this much she knew, and probably a little intimidating, considering Olivia's little gasp when they first entered the room. His hand had been firm, but very gentle, and she imagined they were callused from honest work. His face would be tanned from hours in the sun and wind, and his body lean and muscular. He was still young, she surmised since he had moved with a younger man's speed and agility. Handsome, she decided that his hair was dark brown to match his eyes. She smiled at her foolish fantasy. Likely he was missing teeth, with a portly belly and bald. Not that it mattered in her consideration of him. If all went well, he would be her knight in shining armor before the day was over.

The carriage pulled to a stop, and Claire became aware or the strong salty sea air. "Here you be, miss," a gruff voice announced from the driver's seat.

"Can you assist me down and to the gangplank, please?" Claire asked, trying to hold fast onto her image of the kind captain.

With a maximum amount of grumbling, 'good old Jim' came round to assist her, not entirely paying attention to his customer. Jim seemed oblivious of her shortcomings, and shared his opinion that 'high class ladies' were a weak lot that probably needed a man to walk them to the window to see if the day was clear. "There you are! Berth 7, the *RavenSong* by the looks of her and I've walked you to the entryway. Now, how about you pay your fare, and let a man return to his living?"

His complaints helped to soothe her nerves, and Claire kept her eyes downcast so that she could enjoy his disregard. Better that he easily forget just another 'weak high class lady' than remember the blind woman traveling without escort asking for Berth 7. She held out the fare and a modest tip for his 'kind service', and then turned to square her shoulders and face the last and highest hurdle to freedom and Edward.

*   *   *

The scent of roses was intoxicating in the confined space, and Olivia gasped as Philip Trent, the seventh Lord Forthglade, pressed her against the arrangement table with his own hard length. The room swam as he traced hot kisses down her throat while skillful hands caressed the hardened peaks of her breasts through the thin silk of her décolletage. A soft

Blind Aphrodite

moan escaped her lips, as one manicured hand left its work to begin to trace the line of her legs, skimming along the curve of her inner thigh.

"Shhh, my tigress," he crooned against her skin, feeling her shiver at the sensation of warm breath against the hollow of her throat. "We wouldn't want to be indiscreet, now would we?"

"No, of course not," she pushed against him, only too aware of just how far he would be willing to go before allowing reason to rule. He loved the danger of these secret trysts, and thrived on the delicious thrill of pleasuring her scant feet away from 'respectable society'. Payments to Monsieur Joubert ensured that their weekly meetings would remain uninterrupted and undiscovered, but Philip had been known to improvise— always finding a willing and passionate accomplice in Olivia. Her cheeks still warmed to recall a spring ball for Claire, where Philip had made love to her for the first time in a curtained alcove. He had held his hand over her mouth to smother her cries as she climaxed while prissy Lady Delaford and her virginal daughter sat gossiping and complaining only two feet away. It had been that same fateful night that they had devised their plan to be together and a flush-faced Olivia had introduced a blind Claire briefly to Lord Forthglade.

Thoughts of Claire sobered Olivia quickly and she pushed a little harder to make sure that Philip was also brought into the present. "I cannot let you distract me, my darling. Our quarry is within reach, and timing is critical."

Philip reluctantly released her, forcing his gaze up from the rosy tip that had escaped the confines of her dress. He let go, but decided that such an open bid for attention could not be ignored. One last kiss on its pouting tautness, and he stepped back looking as innocent as a schoolboy. "Olivia, you really should relax. Claire isn't going anywhere, and it is cruel of you to leave me in such a state." He took her hand to guide her towards the evidence of his need, but Olivia was not to be dissuaded. She snatched her hand away and gave him her sweetest smile.

"Philip, my goal is to never leave you in such a state ever again. And once Claire accepts your marriage proposal, followed quickly by the wedding and her demise, you will have seen the last of my cruelty. At least, as far as you're concerned."

"You are an astonishing woman, Olivia Kent." His wicked smile was a mate to her own.

"Why, thank you, Lord Forthglade," she gave him a mocking curtsey, making sure her ample bosom was displayed to its best advantage. "And when I am Lady Forthglade, you can forget every thought of marital boredom you ever entertained."

He stifled a laugh, enjoying the promises she made. Olivia was as sexually voracious as he was, and he had no doubt she proved a good match for his appetite and style. But as for becoming the next Lady Forthglade, he kept his thoughts to himself on that score. For now, it was all about securing Claire's vast fortune and ensuring that his family didn't follow the path that Olivia's had. Her greed matched his, and he used it to maneuver her towards his goal. In the meantime, he did his best to appear biddable. "You win, tigress. What next?"

"You will send another 'heartfelt' marriage proposal, and this time, you'll be accepted! There's no time to waste with her uncle failing quickly. She will agree because I will have her convinced that it will be the only way to comfort her dying uncle."

"And if he dies before she does?"

"Then the guilt of knowing that she denied his last wishes will seal her fate."

"You are a very clever girl, my tigress," the warmth ignited again in his eyes.

More clever than you realize, Philip. You marry her, and keep separate rooms. And when she dies, I'll make sure to keep some piece of evidence that ties you to her death. Insurance, my darling, that you won't turn on me once the money is in your hands. "Not clever, my darling, just practical."

Blind Aphrodite

"Then come give practical relief to a dying man," he tried to draw her back into his arms with every intention of being indiscreet.

"I've taken far too much time already, my love. Claire will have gathered an entire field of useless flowers by now—and I want to keep a close eye on her in the next few days. Remember, you write the note today and send it immediately. If all goes according to plan, you'll be a groom and then a widower before the month is out."

"Well, on that note, I should take my leave. However, next week you'll not sidestep me so easily. I shall be too hungry for foolish chatter, dearest." His eyes smoldered and she felt another shiver run through her at the mental image of what his hunger entailed and she felt her own desire sing in agreement.

"No chatter," she whispered as he tipped his hat and disappeared out the shop's back door. With a firm shake she forced herself not to run after him, but instead started to brush out her skirts and then moved towards a rusty tin plate hanging over a workbench. The dim and spotted reflection wouldn't do for serious repairs, but she could at least ensure that her hair ornament wasn't askew or that Philip hadn't left any souvenirs on her delicate white skin. He was notorious for 'love tokens' as he called them, and she could only be grateful for Claire's handicap to spare her the trouble of coming up with excuses for them. Luckily, the house servants already knew better than to cross her.

Confident that she showed no evidence from her 'appointment', she hurried back into the main shop floor, remembering at the last to snatch up a large handful of gladiolas so that Claire wouldn't have any suspicions. Philip's playfulness had caused time to slip past her at an alarming rate, but she was sure Claire wouldn't have any objections. Weeks ago, Claire had made an idle comment once that Olivia seemed to take a good deal of time with her selections. But Olivia had shamed her to silence by noting how much longer time must seem to the disabled and then apologized profusely for seeking a moment alone amidst all the beauty that Claire was unable to appreciate. It had been one of the first times that Olivia had pulled Claire up short with a cutting comment veiled in concern. Olivia had felt a surge of power, as Claire's stunned expression had become contrition itself.

As she circled the shops narrow aisles for the second time, the first prickle of concern made its presence known. Claire should have been standing near the front window with an armful of mismatched blossoms, but was nowhere to be seen.

Olivia reassured herself that the little fish was probably waiting in the carriage, whining about how her feet hurt, or visiting with Thomas like some common housewife. But the next jolt made her drop her stems as she realized that the carriage was gone! Air seemed to vanish from the shop, and a million scenarios of ruined plans assaulted her reason. Without a moment's hesitation, Olivia rushed from the shop crushing the dropped petals under her feet. She hired a carriage and ordered them to the townhouse.

'What if she came to the back of the shop to look for me and heard our tryst? It's just the kind of thing to panic a stupid blind ninny, so she rushed home. Or word came about her uncle and she couldn't find me, so she just went home. Or…or…the possibilities were endless and Olivia forced herself to be still. She was furious and already composing the dressing down she was going to give Claire for scaring the life out of her. 'That little idiot! She's lucky I need her to get to the money, or I'd strangle her for this.'

Chapter Five

At the foot of the entryway, Claire hesitated. The rope seemed far too unstable a guide, and she now remembered how treacherous the short distance had seemed, even with Olivia holding her steady. Before she thought to recall the driver, the sound of his carriage and horses had faded. Frozen on the docks for only a minute or two, Claire once again tried to summon Edward for strength. But it was Mr. Guilford who appeared as if called.

"All right, then, what mischief brings you back, miss?" he announced as he came down the swaying walk. "You'll not sweet talk past me just to break the captain's heart again, you hear me? Where's the she-dragon?"

She recognized his voice instantly as the gentleman who had allowed them on board yesterday, but his greeting stunned her for its blunt force, as well as its content. After a quick breath to try to make a clean start, she decided that his first comment was the easiest one to address and she would disregard the rest of his playful banter. "No mischief, Mr. Guilford, I can assure you. Only the most urgent business with your Captain Grayson."

"Urgent business?" he sounded unconvinced. "I am trusted with all the Captain's business, so you can tell me first and then I'll decide if he needs to be troubled further."

Whatever calm and courage she had gathered around her in the ride over seemed to dissolve at this unexpected gatekeeper. Worse, the longer she stood there negotiating entrance, the more likely she was to draw attention to the odd sight of a young noblewoman trying to come aboard a trading vessel in broad daylight. Each minute spent was one that she could not regain, and her imagination made every carriage that approached fill with Olivia and the forces to stop her. Gentle pleas would probably get her nowhere, and so out of sheer desperation, she decided another tactic might serve.

"I don't have time for this nonsense, Mr. Guilford." Her tone brooked no arguments and she stiffened her spine in what she hoped was an intimidating manner. "Now, escort me on board to see your Captain immediately, or by this day, I will not be responsible for the welts this stick is likely to raise on your less than bright skull."

She was breathless in shock at her own cheek by the time she finished, convinced he would now throw her bodily into the harbor. Instead, she heard Samson's voice filled with laughter and admiration, "Well, that sounds fairly urgent to me. Right this way, little lady." His arm was steady and he clucked like a mother hen all the way up the ramp. "Of course, I'm regretting this already considerin' the damage you did yesterday to the poor man. But I suppose a little torment is good for the soul, at least that's what them street prophets is always going on about."

She was so grateful to be getting off the dock and out of sight, that his words were lost to her but she managed to offer at least token agreement with his friendly fussing.

Rutger was sure that a night without sleep had somehow caught up with him as the hallucination of Samson escorting Miss Aylesbury on board the *RavenSong* materialized before his eyes. As he crossed the decks, the vision only came closer. She was wearing the softest cream and ivory, a foil for her dark coloring and in the sunlight, he noticed for the first time burgundy streaks in the deep ebony of her curls.

"Now, Captain, before you get angry, she threatened to clout me if I didn't let her back on board."

Blind Aphrodite

Rutger's reply died in this throat as the softest peach blush touched her cheeks at Samson's jest. *Oh god, she's done it again and I just managed to convince myself that she wasn't this beautiful, and that I wasn't this stupid.*

"Captain Grayson," she extended her hand, misdirected by several inches this time by his silence. "I realize this is awkward, but could I please speak with you again privately?" She gave him a hesitant smile, unaware of his inner turmoil.

"Of course," he recovered his voice just in time, "Right this way." He took the hand she offered and wrapped it easily around his arm to guide her into the companionway. He was aware of every step, announcing each turn to avoid causing her to stumble. In the few seconds it took to reach his quarters, the scent of her hair and skin was burned into his memory for all time. Rutger found himself praying that she had another simple letter for him to read and that she would be gone quickly before he needed to be committed to bedlam.

He directed her to sit and then tried to brace himself for whatever she might say as he took his own seat. "Is there something I can do for you, Miss Aylesbury?"

She lifted her gaze to his face, and he wondered if she was aware of how much her eyes conveyed. It was like watching a beautiful storm gather, and he was hypnotized by its strength.

"I need your help to look for my brother, and I believe, in doing so you may save my life." It hadn't been the request he had expected—Rutger sat in stunned silence as she continued.

"There isn't much time, and if they find me, I have no doubt that there won't be another opportunity to escape. I know this sounds insane. Believe me, I hear myself, and I can't believe the words. But I trust you with my life and now with Edward's."

"They?" he probed carefully, trying to understand exactly what kind of enemies she possessed.

"I'm not sure, but my uncle is dying and has been manipulated into either seeing me wed to an odious man or institutionalized 'for my own good' before he passes. Or at least that's what Olivia has conveyed. And how can I trust the woman who read Edward's last letter a hundred times but never once mentioned his whereabouts? Who befriended me, but now seems to control my every movement? They've trapped me like a blind animal," her voice broke, but she continued on in a rush, "The only one who would have prevented this would have been Edward, and now he has mysteriously disappeared."

"And you're convinced that he is alive?"

"Captain Grayson, Edward is alive, and if I can find him then everything can be set to rights."

"You want me to go to Savannah and find your brother?" He felt himself already agreeing to the quest. A fool's errand, but he doubted that there was anything he wouldn't do for her at this point. But her reply froze him in his chair.

"No, Captain Grayson. I want you to take me to Savannah to find my brother." Head held high; she said it simply and then quietly waited for his response, like a prisoner awaiting the judge's final verdict.

The moment spun out between them. It didn't matter if the danger were real or imagined. It was real to her, and something in him recognized her terror as genuine. The ship was his to direct where he willed, and if her brother were alive then it would be an additional bonus to a likely lucrative trade run to supply the British army. Or at least that was the practical excuse he would repeat to himself over and over to justify this instant of complete lunacy. There was really no choice to be made.

"When would you like to set sail?" he heard himself ask her calmly.

"Oh!" tears came now, and she rose without thinking. "How can I ever thank you for everything?" She came around the small table easily, her fingers gliding along the edge effortlessly, and found herself hugging her newfound savior from sheer joy and relief. "Thank you, Captain Grayson!"

Blind Aphrodite

When he was sure his heart would simply stop beating as a hundred sensations coursed through what he considered an already overtaxed nervous system, he gently removed his tearful, inaugural passenger. "There now, Miss Aylesbury. No thanks are necessary. But when did you want to sail?"

"Immediately. I can pay my way, of course." She reached into her reticule and managed to shock him yet again by fishing out an enormous diamond encrusted necklace. "It was my mother's, so I am sure she wouldn't mind seeing it put to good use."

The necklace glittered in her hand like a jeweled snake, and Rutger was glad for the painful wrench in his midsection at the sight of it. It reminded him of her position and wealth, a trinket she had thrown in her bag that would have purchased his vessel and its contents—a glittering reality he could have once claimed himself. Now it was like a splash of ice water to restore his balance. He would take her to look for her brother for no payment, but if he ever needed to remind himself of a reason for controlling whatever madness she inspired, it was this moment.

"Keep it," he told her quietly.

"I insist on reimbursing you for the voyage. Please—"

"Keep it, for now," he added, wanting to soften his words, "You can always pay me after we find Edward, if you still insist upon it." She smiled and nodded her agreement, placing the priceless bauble back into her handbag.

He continued on, "As for an immediate departure, we'll have to wait a few hours for the tide. And I'll need the time in any case to collect my men from their shore leave and then to stand to."

"A few hours!" fear seized her again, and while she knew it was unreasonable to expect him to just pull up anchor at a moment's notice, she knew Olivia would not be far behind her now.

"Don't panic. Did you leave bags on the dockside?" he deliberately tried to divert her with the practical matters involved with traveling.

Renee Bernard

She blushed again, confessing, "No, I did manage to smuggle a few dresses and items, but I have no bags."

"So, I'm to be harboring a smuggler, am I?"

His teasing tone reminded her of Edward, and Claire found herself warming to her knight more and more by the instant. "If you must know, I tied them to my farthingale so that Olivia wouldn't notice them."

"Ah! A talented and imaginative smuggler! I shall have to ask you to curtail your criminal activities while on board my ship, please. I wouldn't want to see you keel-hauled, Miss Aylesbury." Her laughter made him feel immensely pleased. Apparently the ability to flirt and make polite conversation didn't exactly disappear without practice—it just raised its rusty head long enough to make a man wish for days gone by. "Well, let's address the issue of accommodations."

"Do you have guest quarters?" she asked innocently.

It was his turn to blush, "The *RavenSong* is many things, but I'm afraid she isn't a passenger ship. Which suits your purposes, since no one will suspect you of choosing this vessel to take you to the colonies. I know it would seem the logical choice to offer you these quarters, but this room also serves as the officer's mess and the charting and records room." Rutger considered his options, trading accommodations or moving some of the men, but he feared that a woman on board was enough adjustment for one voyage without disrupting the crew's small comforts. Just then his eyes lit on the smaller door leading off from his quarters, "Ah! Problem solved. There is a smaller room, but still a comfortable one off of my own you can use. It was designed for a cabin boy, or second mate, but Samson hates enclosed spaces and after the—," Rutger caught himself out of instinct, and hoped she hadn't noticed. "So I've just used it for storage. That is…if you don't mind the proximity." Rutger felt his face turn several shades of red.

"The proximity?" she asked, unsure of his meaning, but sensing that she had just missed a turn in the conversation.

Blind Aphrodite

"It opens into this room only, and not onto the companionway. I'll of course have Samson put a lock on the door if that will make you feel more comfortable."

"That will be fine." She smiled at the mental image of her now gallant knight trying to protect her virtue. She held no fears of Capt. Grayson or his crew, only of the dragons on shore. "A lock seems unnecessary, but perhaps for decorum's sake."

"Here, I'll show you to your quarters while we make preparations to leave." As he navigated the room, he instinctively named the objects they moved to avoid, "Large table here, you can tell you are near it when the carpet begins. Now past the stove, which remains cold in this season so don't worry to touch it and here are my books and you can feel along the wall with this hand railing to the door. It's a low beam, but I'm actually the one who needs to duck, so you should be fine."

Her room was small, but efficient. Boxes and light equipment were stacked against one wall, but it was otherwise clean. Like the captain's quarters, it had the advantage of a multi-paned window that could be opened for a breeze, or allow for light to give its occupant cheer. A tiny window seat with drawers beneath, a chipped washstand and a single narrow bunk were its only furnishings.

"A window! How wonderful!" Claire exclaimed, hands outstretched to touch its clear diamond shaped panes.

"You can see the window?" Rutger felt his heart lurch, with both hope and fear.

She turned to him with a delighted smile, "I can see some bright lights, but only to tell me a direction of the source. Of course on a sunny day, then the world is just one horribly white blur filled with black streaks. For the most part, I am in the dark as one would imagine, and lights are just gray marks to help my bearings."

A million questions leapt to his mind about her affliction and its cause, but he said only "I'd forgotten the room had a window, so I'm glad you can enjoy it." He made sure she knew where everything was, and promised to have the equipment removed as soon as possible. "Is there anything else you'll need, or anything special you require before we get underway?"

"No, you've been too kind," Claire's eyes filled with tears, robbing her of his outline against the bright square of light.

"Not at all. Stay here until we're underway, and I'll fetch you when it's safe. In the meantime, try to make yourself comfortable, and I'll send Samson in with a lunch tray for you." He paused, unsure what else to say or how he might make her feel less terrified. As he ducked through the door, he cursed himself for being a mannerless oaf and closed it tight behind him.

*   *   *

"We're leaving on the next high tide." Rutger disregarded the shocked look on Samson's face, "Call the men back immediately, and send Mallory to fetch these items. I want to see Mr. Cutter as soon as he's back aboard." He handed Samson the list that would reveal all.

"Bolt lock, tea, a set of silk bed sheets, feather pillows, extra—omigod, you're kidnapping her!"

"Hardly," Rutger's wry response, unable to look directly at his old friend. "I've agreed to help her look for her missing brother, so Miss Aylesbury will be traveling with us for a while." He turned back, meaning to give Samson a stern lecture on a captain's prerogative when he saw the look on Samson's face. It was an odd mix of horror and resignation.

"I'd follow you to hell, Muck my friend. I suppose, we can all take a quick trip to Savannah to help a damsel in distress. But, are you sure this is something you want to do to yourself? Why not refer her to another ship's captain you trust to take her? Or help her get a ticket on a regular passenger sailing vessel?"

Blind Aphrodite

Rutger considered the questions, all so sincere and logical. "Because she asked me to take her. Because I would never stop worrying about her if I didn't, and because I can at least protect her while she's on board. Because I'm an idiot and it's worth any price to be able to just sit with a woman again and have her laugh at one of my jokes." He stopped himself, knowing he'd already said too much, but unable to take it back.

Without another word, Samson took his friend's arm in a gesture that said a great deal about his concern and his support. He nodded, and left to carry out his captain's orders and start getting the vessel underway.

"One more thing, Samson," Rutger caught up with him at the head of the quarterdeck. "I'll have a quick meeting with our officers on deck before we sail to ensure that there aren't any misunderstandings."

"Anything else, Captain?"

"You'll see to it that no one calls me 'Muck' in her presence." It was almost a whisper.

"You didn't even have to ask," and Samson left him to his thoughts

*   *   *

Claire sat on the edge of her little bunk, having already put away the few items she managed to smuggle on board into the clever little drawers underneath the window seat. There was little to do, but listen to the sounds of the men working on the decks and loading the last of the supplies. She was unable to relax, still waiting for some alarm, or for Captain Grayson to come back and tell her he'd changed his mind about this misguided adventure.

She heard the captain call out an order to the linesman, and her heart flip-flopped a little. She attributed her feelings to his ready agreement to take her, and then a dozen subtle courtesies he had shown her—narrating the room, or just the way he guided her down the companionway without really seeming to steer or fuss. He made her forget the darkness, and when she had impulsively embraced him something in her had shifted. Unfamiliar warmth had enfolded her as she unconsciously took in his height and broad shoulders, the muscular wall of his chest and the feel of his silk shirt and jacket beneath her cheek. He was clean-shaven because she had felt no whiskers bump against the top of her head or face. His scent was a sweet mixture of soap and wood, salt and sandalwood. It seemed her imagination had done no justice to the reality of the man.

She wondered if he thought her attractive at all, and then pushed the idea away quickly. Her own looks, or lack of them, was not something she could solve. Olivia had told her that she was attractive, if somewhat plain. Besides, romance was the last thing on her mind these days. Finding Edward and escaping whatever plans had been laid out for her—this was the goal. Captain Grayson had simply offered her a means to achieve it. Besides, a man of action could hardly be bothered with a blind runaway heiress. Could he?

Chapter Six

◯

Olivia was furious—she experienced a rage that made her feel as if her flesh were woven of fire. They had lost over an hour with the bizarre mix-up of the misdirected carriage. That Claire had deliberately lied and sent Thomas off on a fool's errand was confounding for Olivia. She had heard stories of Claire's cleverness as a young girl, and had even admired her spirit a bit when they had first met. But her lost sight had given Olivia a ready tool and Claire had been easily cowed and manipulated. As far as Olivia could tell, this strange turn of events was like a bolt of lightning on a clear day. She had never seen it coming. A blind woman, alone, to just run—without warning and apparently with just the clothes on her back.

"Oh my! Whatever shall we tell his Grace?" the quavering whine of Mrs. Mills, the housekeeper, refocused Olivia instantly. Eyes of ice swept over the weeping woman, hiding none of the contempt Olivia felt at this moment.

"You shall tell him nothing, if you don't want to find yourself on the streets, old woman," Olivia's voice was the hiss of a venomous snake, and Mrs. Mills' tears froze in their greasy tracks. "I know exactly where Miss Claire is headed, and it is only a matter of a few hours before she is home safe and sound. There is no need to upset His Grace, or worse, to tire him needlessly with this childish prank."

"Y—you know where she is?" Mrs. Mills croaked, unsure of the proper response to either the information or the open fury.

"See to your duties, Mrs. Mills, and I will see to mine," the calm fury in her voice drove the timid housekeeper out without another second of hesitation.

The carriage ride to Lord Forthglade's brownstone gave Olivia time to feel her anger settle into a churning mass in her stomach. She had realized quickly that she couldn't act alone in her search, and so had decided to make her way towards her only ally. As her hand closed over the heavy brass knocker on the forbidding front door, it occurred to her that Philip might not even be home. She had no idea of where he went after their weekly rendezvous. The butler's eyes gave nothing away, but admitted her without protest. She was instructed to wait in a small sitting room while Lord Forthglade was informed of her arrival.

She had only been to the house once several weeks ago. As she waited, the memory washed over her. Philip's cousin, Miss Florence Drake, had been visiting for a shopping excursion, and Claire had been invited over to a tea. She knew that it was entirely Philip's doing, a chance for him to play his dangerous games. He had greeted her as if they were strangers, and then moved away to pay his polite compliments to Claire. Olivia had been forced to make inane conversation with a decrepit grand dame, all the while trying not to feel the heat he evoked in her. She had been sure that he had been foiled in his illicit plans as the formal tea kept all the ladies confined in the salon. At least until his cousin had suggested that they move to the adjoining garden for a stroll. The weather had been extremely fine, and even Claire had shyly agreed that a walk would be refreshing. The small group fractured to follow different paths and she and Claire made their way to a cluster of willows where there was a small wrought iron seat. She had settled Claire in to enjoy the breeze and then caught sight of Philip watching from the windows. She excused herself to return to the house for her shawl, and slipped back into the house. In the very room where the cream of London's most high-minded society had just set

Blind Aphrodite

down their china tea cups, Philip had bent her over the brocade sofa and plundered her body until she cried against the pillows. The encounter had taken only minutes, but Olivia remembered the dark, delicious shiver that ran through her when she realized as she was straightening her skirts from having been pushed over her head, that the cups had been cleared away. It was then she understood the depths of Philip's depravity, and her own.

"Reminiscing my dear?" his voice was biting, but still a welcome sound to Olivia's overwrought nerves. "After all the effort we expend to be discreet, isn't this forward of you, Miss Kent?"

"Something has happened. Claire has disappeared and I'm afraid she has gone to look for Edward. It has only been a couple of hours, so I'm sure if we search the docks for passenger vessels to the colonies and alert the port authorities to look for a blind—"

"Don't be foolish, Olivia," Philip cut her off with a soft growl, "The last thing you want is to explain to someone in authority who your charge is and how you managed to lose her. Besides, you said she had no idea where Edward is. So how is it she is suddenly bound for the Americas?"

"She must have had the letter with her when we—it doesn't matter now." She stopped herself as his expression changed.

"Not such a clever tigress, after all?" His eyes glittered at her for another instant and then he turned to pour himself a brandy, his pace completely unhurried.

"Philip, we have to catch her!" Olivia was astonished at his relaxed manner, but also wary of the twists and turns of his mind.

"And we will, dearest," he moved to settle onto an elegant chair, enjoying the sight of Olivia off-balance and confused. He considered it payback for her teasing love-play earlier in the day. Not a full payment, but he would have that soon enough. "She has just done us a great favor, by allowing us to write the rest of the drama."

"I—I don't understand. A favor?" she felt as if she had missed some crucial exchange in a conversation, and now sought desperately to find the correct threads of logic in his words.

"Yes, you see, we just eloped, Claire and I," his smile made her heart lurch in astonishment. "I will leave a few choice notes about how we just couldn't wait another day to be together, her uncle's endless illness, Edward's disappearance, etc. and have run off."

"But you haven't gone anywhere."

"We'll leave right away, and the illusion will be complete. We simply go fetch her and when Edward tells her exactly what we want him to tell her, she falls into my sympathetic arms and we marry, return to London just in time for an accident or a debilitating illness to make you and I extremely rich and happy."

Just as the endless protests against this amazing plan began to spring to her lips, one word struck her breathless, "We?"

"Too much chatter, blossom," his tone was familiar black velvet, and all talk of schemes and illusions fell away. "You promised that the next time we met, there would be no foolish chatter. Come and pay your debts."

Olivia stood without another word and crossed to kneel in front of his chair, needing no instructions on the kind of payment that would satisfy him. It was a payment that would satisfy them both.

Chapter Seven

∽

Rutger's concerns about his crew's reactions to a woman on board the *RavenSong* had been for naught. None of the men had made any comments regarding their captain's odd behavior or the sudden change of plans. Instead, they had almost immediately decided to adopt her as a beloved mascot, and despite all of Rutger's admonitions to the crew to treat Miss Aylesbury with the utmost courtesy, the men insisted on affectionately calling her Lady Claire, or even the Captain's Lady Claire when she wasn't present. It was almost comical to see a ship of rough and hardy men turn into barefoot courtiers overnight. He suspected that by the end of their first day at sea, they were most of them already half-sick with calf-love, himself included.

Her tiny room had been transformed before they left port, and Rutger knew he would have draped the room in gold for her comfort if necessary. A soft woven rug, silk bedding, and even a cushion for her window seat were added, but Rutger had been unable to stop himself at what he considered minimal improvements. Mallory had been mystified by the shopping list his captain had provided, but had brought back a wide array of ladies toiletry items, including perfumed soaps and lotions, tortoise shell hair combs and even sachets for the drawers.

Claire had been unable to hide her delight at his generous efforts on her behalf, blushing at his 'thoughtfulness' and pleading to pay him for the items. Rutger's face colored recalling just how she had unknowingly paid him in that instant—standing next to him, her hand on his arm to steady herself against the ship's gentle rolling motion. Her eyes held only pleasure at the gifts as she looked up into his face, and Rutger had decided that no matter the outcome, the price would have been worth it. Desire surged through him in the confined space, less than two strides away from silken sheets and then, he had made some quick excuse to escort her above decks for a breath of fresh air.

Routines developed quickly at sea and even Cutter, the ship's physician, made the offhand comment that a lady's hands seem to make the ocean a little smoother. According to custom, each morning the officers gathered at the large table in his quarters for breakfast and a debriefing. What had always been a simple meal, peppered with ship's business and male camaraderie, now became a bright highlight in the officers' day. Lady Claire joined them, unknowingly taking a significant chair to the Captain's right, at Samson's insistence. She was fascinated by their stories, and interested and curious to understand the ship's workings and their own roles aboard the *RavenSong*. Rutger had been pleased at their efforts, if not altogether perfected, at gentlemanly conversation and table manners.

They vied for her attention and smiles, and from Samson down to his lowliest deckhand, they all seemed to keep a sharp eye out for her safety. The RavenSong's walkways had never been so clear of clutter. If Rutger had worried her lack of sight would make time pass more slowly for their passenger, he had not accounted for a crew determined to keep 'their Lady Claire' entertained. Sailor's tales, somewhat censored for a lady's ears, were regaled at will. Mallory offered to teach her to fish, and Samson had even offered to show her how to make sailor's knots and ties. But some things were reserved for Rutger, and he looked forward to his own daily highlights with the Lady Claire, their sunset walks and dinner alone in his quarters with lively debates on politics, philosophy or whatever suited their mood.

Blind Aphrodite

As the late afternoon sun began the final stage of its fall into the seas, Rutger left the ship's wheel in Mr. Sweet's capable hands and made his way to his quarters. He knocked on the door briefly, and heard Claire's call to come in. Rutger opened the door expecting to see her waiting for him. Confusion crossed his features as the door opened on what appeared to be an empty room.

"Miss Aylesbury?" he asked uncertainly, eyes scanning the interior quickly.

"Oh! I am here, Captain!" Claire sat up quickly from her position on the floor. She was on her knees next to one of the two great ceiling support columns.

Rutger was at her side instantly, sure that she was injured, "Did you fall? Are you hurt?" his voice was almost curt in its concern.

Her laugh was rich and sweet in his ears, "No, of course not! I was just admiring the carvings, and am embarrassed to say, you have caught me in a most undignified position!"

"Not exactly undignified," he countered with a sigh of relief, "You just weren't in the position I'd expected. Here, let me help you to your feet."

She had abandoned her gloves and he felt the touch of his bare hands to hers for the first time. It was a minor detail that most seamen wouldn't notice, but for Rutger the connection of his rough hands against hers was profound. His imagination made it seem as if her fingers trembled against his, perhaps from the same sensations, but he dismissed the thought quickly. She rose easily, and he tried to ignore the loss of his hand holding hers, only to feel her sway and nearly stumble against him.

Rutger caught her quickly "Did you stand up too fast?" He held both her arms for balance until he felt her regain her equilibrium. A voice inside his head said that a gentleman would put her hand against the post for balance and then step away, but Rutger preferred his first instincts.

The sensation seemed to pass quickly, and Claire grinned up at him, "Yes, I suppose I was down there longer than I realized. I'm determined to prove to you what a good sailor I can be."

"I'm already impressed," his simple compliment was not lost, as he saw its meaning register in her telling gaze. Although, he doubted that anything he said could match a single London season of endless flattery. He watched the play of thoughts and emotions in her face. She looked simultaneously pleased and puzzled.

"What are you thinking, Miss Claire?" his voice's soft probe made her realize that she had forgotten herself completely.

"I was thinking about all the work that must have gone into these carvings," she answered evasively, the lie clumsy on her lips.

"I see," he moved to her side, letting her keep her secrets. "Did you find the salamanders hiding in the leaves?"

Her face lit up at his diversion, "No! Can you show them to me?"

"I suppose so. Although I should probably just let you search for them on your own. It *is* a long voyage," he teased, relishing the casual banter.

"I suppose you could," she countered, "If you didn't mind me pestering you endlessly, I can be a very persistent woman."

"All right, then, I yield," he gave in easily, "Here, let me show you my hidden roommates." They moved to the first post, and he guided her hands along the curve of one vine. "Do you feel it? His tail is wrapped around the base of that flower, and then he peeks out from between these two leaves. He is level with your eyes." It was the sweetest torture, and he wondered what kind of fool plays at games he knows he will lose. As Claire laughed to discover the ring of creatures hidden on the post, he tried to greedily memorize every detail, his eyes ranging over her unchecked.

In showing her the carvings, he now stood close enough to breathe in the perfumed scent of her hair. Without the help of a ladies maid, she had pulled it back in a simple twist, ebony curls cascading from the back with one stray spiral falling forward across her shoulders to trail over the generous swell of her breasts. Rutger's throat tightened as he realized that he could simply pull one hairpin, and the entire mass would fall down her

Blind Aphrodite

back. Her gown was elegant in its simplicity, wedgewood blue silk, without any useless ruffles and decorations, it only accented her feminine curves and inherent beauty. She glanced at him innocently, hoping for more secrets, and he tried to ignore his body's thickening reaction to her movement and the way she unconsciously leaned against him.

"Are all the posts in the room carved like this?" she asked him breathlessly.

"Even the bed posts," Rutger's glib answer was past his lips before he knew it, and at her small gasp, he knew he had overstepped himself. "Shall we take that walk on deck, Miss Aylesbury?" He moved quickly, trying to escape his awkward slip. She nodded assent, and as he escorted her from the room, even as he wondered if Cutter had brought anything on board that would help him sleep nights.

As they began their walk, Claire tried to keep her eyes downcast, struggling to regain her internal balance. Captain Grayson seemed to be able to make her head swim simply by touching her hand. She couldn't recall a single instant when a man had affected her the way Rutger did. She hoped that she hadn't made a fool of herself in his cabin just then. She couldn't seem to make herself stop touching him, or leaning against him. She could feel herself aching to cling to him, like one of those sinuous carved vines. In barely ten days aboard the *RavenSong*, he had become the center of her thoughts. He was at once, familiar and mysterious—someone she felt as if she had always known, but knew nothing about. When she should have been thinking only of Edward and the reason for her journey, she could only think about this man she longed to hold and who made her feel like a queen aboard his ship. Rutger supported her without making her feel dependent, and had anticipated so many of her requirements, that she had never had to make an awkward plea for assistance. How was it possible that a complete stranger had put so much effort towards offering her independence?

Of one thing, she was certain. Her heart seemed to have a momentum of its own, and after years of letting everyone else set her course, she was determined to follow her own path. Like the salamanders, she wondered if her own happiness wasn't within her reach if she just knew where to look for it.

They strolled along the deck without speaking at first, and Claire realized that Capt. Grayson was matching his stride to hers as she measured her paces to familiarize herself with the Song.

"The *RavenSong* is very beautiful, Captain Grayson," Claire confided as they stopped along the rail.

"I'm flattered that you think so," his words were tinged with pride.

"I hadn't realized that ships had such fine woodwork inside them. Samson said even the men's quarters have bookshelves and inset private storage spaces."

"Not all ships share the Song's amenities," he responded, "I confess I am very proud of her comforts. When you live on a ship, it seems to make sense that you would want to make it as much like a home as possible."

"The carvings remind you of home?" she asked, hoping he wouldn't find her question too intrusive.

His hesitation was palpable, and just as she was about to interject an apology for her rudeness, his reply carried to her on the early evening breeze. "I missed seeing the gardens of England. I suppose I wanted to take a little beauty of the land with me to sea, and this way the flowers will never fade or wilt."

"How remarkable," Claire felt a lump in her throat at the unexpressed pain behind his words. She looked towards the fading blur of now just gray light in the black void of her field of vision, and thought she understood something of wanting to keep a token to always remind you of better days.

A soft silence fell between them as the sun edged into the sea.

"Captain?"

"Yes?"

Blind Aphrodite

"Would you tell me how the sea and sky look just now?" she waited, trusting him not to mock her simple request.

She heard him take a deep breath, as he paused to compose his thoughts. "The sun has just fallen beneath the horizon, but its rays color the sky. It ranges from a deep periwinkle blue, then to shell pink and fuchsia and orange that is tinged with red. The sea reflects all of those colors, but seems to be drinking them into the depths. The sea grows darker by the moment, and the sky—" A small laugh broke off his prose, "I am no poet, Miss Aylesbury, and I fear I've just ruined the entire event for you."

"Not at all!" she protested, "That was wonderful—until you laughed."

The smile faded from his voice, "Have you ever seen a sunset, Miss Claire?"

"Yes," Claire thought it was perhaps the most sensitive way anyone had ever asked about her blindness. She turned back to face him and felt anew a sense of total trust. "You can ask me anything you wish, if you want to."

"How did you lose your sight?" his tone was even and solemn.

"A fever, over two years ago." She smiled to reassure him, "I wish I could tell you that I was spectacularly brave, but I was a brat for weeks until Olivia forced me to go on with my life." At Olivia's name, she felt her spirits waver, but she shook off any thoughts of her betrayer.

"Doesn't it trouble you?" he sounded mystified.

"Not really." Her brow furrowed as she considered the best way to make him understand, "It is limiting. I do miss my sight, but I fight frustration more than I struggle with self-pity."

"Frustration to not be able to do the things that you want to do?" he asked.

"Frustration that I still feel the same in every way, but that the world doesn't want to treat me the same." Claire leaned back against the railing as she spoke, "Can you imagine what it is like to walk about and feel that without a single exchange, you are judged solely on your limitations? People don't even see me. They just see a 'blind woman', and then they stop looking. As if my life and personality were defined by such a thing! A condition of fate, something completely beyond my control, and everything else that I am or that I ever could be is ignored and discounted. Can you imagine such a thing?"

Emotion shook her voice, and she suddenly wanted more than anything to be held by him. And then the space between them was gone, and she felt comforting arms encircle her, sheltering her against the wall of his broad chest. Tears that had spilled down her cheeks unheeded were wiped gently away, and Claire tipped her head back to thank him—when she became aware of her desire for more than tender sympathy. The ache was so strong that a small moan escaped her parted lips.

And then his lips were on hers, a kiss that was soft and sweet at first, the first silken touch a whisper of passion that deepened to take everything that she instinctively offered him. Claire had never been kissed before, and after only an instant of shock, matched the movements of his tongue with a hunger of her own. Fingers that had clutched at his lapels now splayed to take in the hard lines of his chest and move across his shoulders. Wherever his hand moved across her back, her skin pulsed in reaction. His hand on her face dropped to form a seductive trail down the column of her throat and then circled to trace the sensitive hollow of her neck. She trembled under his hands, maddened by the slow movements of his fingers, only to feel the trail lead further down past the open expanse of her décolletage. Firm fingers swept over the curve of her breast, and she felt her knees melt and disappear as the textured pad of his thumb brushed over its hardened crest through layers of soft silk. Heart pounding, Claire knew that at some point she was supposed to end this, but beyond the rush of blood in her ears and the feel of his arms, she couldn't remember why. The taste of him intoxicated her, as warmth uncoiled inside her forcing another soft groan of pleasure from her lips.

The sound was Rutger's undoing, as she arched her back to press against him, innocently urging him on. Discovering a discipline within

Blind Aphrodite

himself he hadn't realized before, he forced himself to end the kiss. As gently as he could, he disengaged from the embrace even as his body cried out in protest. Hands gripping her shoulders, Rutger closed his eyes to focus on the sound of his own ragged breathing trying to compose any semblance of rational thought. He had been only seconds away from lifting her off her feet to take her to bed, and even now he fought the primal need that screamed at him after endless months of denial.

He opened his eyes and made a quick assessment of the damage he had wrought. Dusk had just fallen, and the lanterns were as yet unlit, so he could only pray the shadows had been enough to hide his folly and to protect her from the eyes of the crew. Her breathing was equally hurried, and her expression was only just clearing of the effects of their kiss. He released his hold on her and stepped back. From ancient experience, Rutger knew that if he didn't supply justification for his actions quickly, Claire would make her own horrible assumptions. With his heart in his mouth, he decided he had no choice but to plunge ahead, "Miss Aylesbury—how can you ever forgive me?" Rutger clenched his jaw in frustration and self-hate, desperate to avoid causing her any pain. "You must think me the most horrendous cad—and I have no defense for my actions."

"No—you were not alone in—"

He didn't need lanterns to see the color that flooded her cheeks, "Please! Don't apologize!"

"But I cannot allow you to take the blame!" Claire stretched out a hand, just as the lanterns from the quarterdeck blazed to life, and illuminated her face and form. She was unaware of the picture she now presented.

Rutger felt as if he had taken a blow to his midsection. She was impossibly beautiful, her hair had fallen in a dark cloud down her back, and her lips were swollen from the force of his touch. Raw emotion choked him, "You offered your trust and I repay you by insulting you on the open deck of my ship." He took a deep breath, "I will have Mr. Mallory see you back to the cabin and bring your dinner. I can assure you, you will not be disturbed again." He turned on his heels without waiting for a reply, and left an astonished Claire standing by the railing with one slender hand still outstretched towards his retreating back.

Chapter Eight

∞

Alone in his quarters, Claire explored the room aimlessly trying to find some small comfort as she ran her fingertips across its furniture and contents. In the last two days, Rutger had managed to avoid her completely. She thought it was no small feat considering the confined spaces aboard the *RavenSong*. The officers had done their best to distract her at breakfast, their awkward silences telling her of their awareness of the strange rift between the pair. She had tried to put on a brave show for them, but at night, there was nothing to distract her from her vigil. She lay in her bunk, listening for any sign of his return in the next room—without success. Last night, she had gathered her courage and actually crept out of her room to try to find him abed. But his bed's broad surface was cold and undisturbed. The temptation to sleep there, in sheets that still held the scents of him, was strong, but Claire finally fled back to her own tiny rest feeling like a complete fool.

Now as she sat at his desk, she despaired of ever making him face her. As she lay her head in her hands, she relived the magical moments on deck when he had taken her into his arms. The power of his kisses had not diminished in the endless hours since he had left her at the rail. Worse, Claire was sure that she was very much in love with her reluctant knight-errant.

She rose impatiently to begin pacing the room. Perhaps it was the blindness that caused him to think her too fragile or incapable of love. She dismissed the theory out of hand. He had never made her feel any less of a human being, and it didn't match his punishing speech. He blamed himself for what he considered an unforgivable breech in protocol. To Claire, his reaction was proof of his honorable nature. Clearly, she had to make him understand that she had been injured in no way, and in fact, considered him her equal.

A knock at the door startled her and she reeled toward the sound, hopeful that Rutger had at last come to talk. She steadied herself with a hand against the 'salamander' post, and called for him to come in.

"Good afternoon, Lady Claire," Mr. Guilford's voice was forcefully cheerful, and Claire did her best to hide her disappointment. "Mr. Cutter is clucking like a mother hen since you're not eating what he feels is a 'proper amount' these days."

"I'm fine," Claire moved to rest at the window seat. "Mr. Cutter is very kind." She wondered if the hollowness she felt was something that Samson could hear.

"Nonsense! He's a tyrant! And said you'd protest and I was to ignore your every word and sit with you until you'd finished every last drop of this hearty broth," Samson moved to set the tray on the table, the clink of silverware making her wince from her lack of appetite.

"He said you are to sit with me?" Claire asked, feeling the first threads of a simple plan fall into place. First mate aboard the *RavenSong*, and a good friend of Rutger by all accounts, Claire decided that if anyone might help her unravel the mystery of her Captain, it was Samson.

"Aye, he did," Samson finished with his table setting, "And I warn you, not even the threat of a good clout on the head will send me off this time."

"Come sit with me then, here for a while. A good conversation to work up an appetite, and I'll be sure to tell Cutter you followed his instructions to the letter," she beckoned him towards a padded chair that sat opposite the window seat. "Tell me, Samson. Have you been aboard the *RavenSong* long?" she began innocently.

Blind Aphrodite

"Since her first days above the waves, Lady," Samson warmed to his topics quickly. "Met Rutger in a tavern brawl and he saved my skull. We shared a pint or two and I learned that the Song had just come into his hands. He needed someone with experience to turn her to good use, and I needed a commission—"

"Came into his hands?" she leaned forward, unable to disguise her interest.

"Consolation inheritance for a fourth son" Samson leaned back, "Don't think it didn't burn him a bit, but he soon fell in love with the life and came to see his father for a wise man. The Song gave him legs to escape the trapped life as one of them society wastrels. Though he did enjoy the best of both worlds for a while," this last ended in a sigh, and Samson seemed to decide there had been enough talk on that subject.

Claire's head was spinning at these revelations, not sure where to head next with her questions, "Have you been traders all these years?"

"Mostly." A curt reply shut the door on the topic.

Claire tried yet another cast of her line fishing for clues about the man whose muffled commands even now rang out on the quarterdeck above her. "Whose initials are B.A.?"

Samson's breath whistled through his teeth, "Where did you hear those?"

"They are carved on a board by my pillow, a crude hand, but it made me wonder."

"Do us all a favor, and don't mention it to the Captain." Samson moved to sit next to her, his voice dropping. "As you well know, the Captain takes a lot onto himself. Amongst ourselves, we've sworn to protect him, but how do you protect a man from himself?"

"Please, Mr. Guilford." She tried not to drop her gaze in embarrassment, hesitant to express her feelings. "I wish to protect him also."

"Benjamin Adams, he was Rutger's first and last cabin boy." Samson kept his voice low, as if wary of being overheard. "Found him stealing to survive off the docks, and Rutger took him in. Doted on him, as we all did. We guessed his age for seven. Bright boy, he would look at you like a bird with the biggest brown eyes you've ever seen. He was a good boy, never had a moment of trouble from him, so eager to please—especially to please Rutger."

"What happened to him?" Claire asked, her throat thick with dread.

"We were genially 'recruited' for a blockade against one of the colonial ports." His voice was sad and bitter, "We should have left the mite behind in England with friends, but we'd been untouchable for so long. Rutger's confidence was boundless, and we set off to show them stupid Yanks what disloyalty to King and Country had bought them."

She wanted him to stop the tale now, but couldn't seem to say anything.

"We were cursed. The winds, the seas, the weather—all against us, when one of the smugglers decided that the Song looked like a weak link in the chain. We took a pounding and lost almost half the crew before it was over. Including Benjie."

"But he couldn't blame himself for an act of war?"

"Couldn't he?" Samson gave a humorless chuckle. "When one of the gunners fell, Benjie had run forward to try to man the cannon himself. Rutger tried to stop him, but not before they were both blown to hell and back."

"Both—" Claire started only to be cut off.

"He convinced himself that it was his arrogance that had taken a child into battle, that if he had left him behind or just locked Benjie safe in the hold when the trouble started—or had a surgeon aboard, or repositioned the ship before the storm struck. It's endless, you see. That night, he lost twenty of the crew he had treated like family. Worse, he lost himself in the aftermath of that battle, and in three years, he has lived with it in every waking moment."

He stood, leaving Claire in stunned silence, as he gathered the tray and she heard him open the window to toss out the now cold broth. Just as he reached the door to leave her to her thoughts, he turned one last time. "He needs you, Lady Claire. I know you've set him on his heels, but he'll come around. Just try to be patient. It's simple really. If he walks away, then he doesn't give you a chance to send him away."

"But that's foolish," she whispered, an ache settling around her heart.

"Nay, that's survival," and he closed the door firmly behind him.

*   *   *

Samson held himself in the hallway for an extra minute, aware of just how far he had gone to betray his friend's trust. His spine stiffened defensively. She hadn't asked about Rutger, just the ship and the boy. Technically, he'd been able to skirt about most of the secrets he had sworn to keep for the Captain. Samson was no fool, for all his easy manners and jolly speeches. Two days of watching his friend prowl about the ship had been enough to convince him that it was time for a little 'divine intervention'. And he was just the bloke to provide it.

He cocked an ear, and waited until he was sure it was Muck's voice coming down the steps, then he began walking out of the companionway to 'bump' into his captain.

"Ahoy! Watch yourself, Captain," Samson jostled the tray as if regaining his balance. "Rutger, you look like hell!"

"A change from my usual appearance in what way?" Biting sarcasm seemed to have no affect on Samson, and Rutger shifted to move past him in the hall's narrow confines.

"No need to growl, friend." Samson continued, dropping his voice in sad resignation, "Just took a tray of broth to the mistress, poor thing." With a sigh, he began to hurry on his way towards the lower decks.

"Wait!" Rutger caught his arm to stop him. "Is she unwell? Have you consulted Cutter?"

"I can't lie to you, Rutger. Cutter's worried." He lifted soulful eyes from the tray, as if hating to be the bearer of this news. "Said her appetite is off and he doesn't like her color one bit." All of which was true, but Samson decided that the rest of what Cutter said about her being fit as a fiddle other than a broken heart, wasn't really relevant to his divine mission.

"Well what the hell is he doing about it?" Golden eyes glittered with concern. A lack of sleep and hours of emotional battery made Rutger impatient and anxious.

Samson's eyes reflected the concern in his captain's face, "Well—he had one suggestion, but…"

"But what? What is it?!" Rutger's anxiety seized him at Samson's uncharacteristic reluctance to talk.

"Cutter said it would be better if someone was closer on hand to keep an eye on her through the night—but the whole crew knows you're avoiding your cabin like the plague." Samson dropped his eyes back to the tray, "Rumor has it you hate her."

Hated her—it was too absurd to put into words. Through clenched teeth he choked out a response to Samson's bizarre allegation, "I most certainly *do not* hate her!"

"Oh," To Rutger's infuriation, Samson did not seem at all convinced. "Good to hear. Poor pretty thing! Of course if you hate her, Mallory would be pleased as punch to stay in your room and tend to her if she—"

"I *don't* hate her!" Rutger's hands balled into fists to keep from throttling his best friend, "And I can certainly sleep in my own cabin or anywhere else on my ship if I damn well want to. Tell Cutter I'll keep an eye out tonight only if he thinks it's really necessary."

"I'm sure he'll be relieved to hear it."

Rutger wheeled away in a fury, and Samson barely managed to wait until he was outside Cutter's door before doing a little jig.

Chapter Nine

I don't hate her. But whatever his feelings, they changed nothing. The game was out of control, and as soon as they touched land, it would be over forever. For now, he would at the very least make sure that she was safe and well for the duration of the voyage. He didn't entirely trust Samson, but Cutter's word was infallible. He had sought out Cutter later that afternoon to confirm the truth of Claire's illness, and the surgeon had repeated his concerns.

So he had waited until he was sure that she had retired for the evening, and then crept quietly into his quarters. In the moonlight, the room was painted in hues of blue and gray, all the colors awash in a scale of shadows. Was this anything like her view of the world? Colorless and strange? He couldn't keep his eyes from seeking the door to her small chamber, or stop himself from imagining the curves of her sleeping form.

The war with his body's frustration raged, and he made his way toward the cold mattress in the great corner bed with condemning thoughts about lying ogres that took advantage of sick, blind women while they slept. He anticipated a long sleepless night spent wrestling with the dilemmas of his own making and listening for any sounds of distress from her door. But as soon as he lay down, tension disappeared and exhaustion pulled him down into the dark weightless fall of dreams.

The RavenSong was on fire. He turned to call out an order to Jenkins to pull hard to starboard, and the main mast exploded in slow motion, sending razor sharp shards across the lower deck. Men pulled at lines that were now tied to burning canvas, and blood began to run across the decks. Rutger shouted again at Jenkins and then ran to try to muster the gun crews to the cannons. One quick glance at the horizon reconfirmed that they had been left to fight alone by an incompetent fleet of British warships. Samson stopped him at the bottom of the stairs, trying to say something about damage to their steering. A small hand tugged at his shirt, and he had waved it away impatiently, screaming at Samson that he had no time to discuss the blasted rudders while the guns sat idle as his men were slaughtered. Another small explosion near the bow, and Rutger fell to his knees—panic and anger making him dizzy.

At the next round of musket fire, he began to move again, unsure of how much time he had lost but now recalling his errand to the gun deck below. The gun deck. Chaos, men wounded and scrambling to push small cannon to their positions, Ellis dead on the floor, and noise he could not absorb or interpret. Benjamin was on the gun deck. Benjamin, with small chubby fingers and a tear streaked face, bravely trying to light one of the fuses. Alone. Rutger ran forward, to see the black powder that had spilt across the floor from a container too heavy for small hands, the fuse that was too short, and the barrel that was too close. To see Benjamin look up at the last to give him a brave smile, to see bright brown eyes filled with trust. To see an explosion that never stopped, a fire that consumed them both in an endless loop of pain. Over and over, he ran across the room, but never in time to stop Benjamin from lowering the torch. Over and over again.

Cool hands smoothed his brow, and Rutger felt his senses return in a rush, his throat raw from screaming at ghosts and the touch of fire he knew all too well. He sat up quickly to brush away the touch, struggling to come to terms with the torturing visions of death that still danced at the edge of his conscious mind and the sweet illusion that was perched on the edge of his bed. She had drawn back the brocade drapery to reach him quickly, and moonlight now flooded around them both. The white silk of

Blind Aphrodite

her dressing gown glowed in the pale shadows, and Rutger thought an angel could not have been more beautiful. But thoughts of saintly creatures fled, as she leaned forward in concern, black curls sliding like a soft curtain behind her, showing him her womanly curves. He found himself inches away from the exposed cream of her face and throat, and wondered if any ogre could withstand this sort of temptation.

He stared into a face outlined by the palest light, her eyes dark reflecting his every thought. Rutger felt something inside of him break loose and decided that he would crown himself king of the ogres to touch her. Later, he would think, but for now, he could only feel.

"Rutger," she said it quietly, making the moment at once surreal and complete for him.

"Claire," he spoke her name possessively, drinking in the taste of it on his lips. Then he reached for her, lifting her easily against him and claimed her healing kisses like a man dying. Her mouth was soft and yielding beneath his, and he plundered the rich sweetness of it, already drunk with the scent of lilacs from her hair and skin. His body hardened with desire, and without thought, he pulled her across his chest to lie underneath him into the great feather-stuffed mattress. With one hand buried in her hair, he urged her to surrender and Claire offered him no resistance. Her mouth clung to his kisses and begged for more.

Her hands covered his chest, seeking to touch his skin. As she skimmed her fingers over his fevered skin, he impatiently shifted to yank off his leather waistcoat and free himself from his white linen shirt in one fluid movement. His eyes never left hers watching the delicious play of innocence and awakening desire in her face as her hands now discovered the firm planes and ridges of his body. Her exploration made his every nerve ending come alive, and he forced himself to hold as still as possible to give her free rein. But as her hand played across the lines of his stomach to reach the barrier of his belt, he knew that he could be still no longer.

Renee Bernard

Rutger whispered her name, hearing a thousand oaths in its single syllable, before surrendering to a primal need to feel her bare skin against his.

Whispered gasps of pleasure sang in his ears as he traced the pulse of her neck with his breath, and his hands began to explore the bounty of curves and hollows. The dressing gown's ties were no defense, and he managed pearl buttons with an expertise he had thought long forgotten. He heard her soft moan as the gown fell open to reveal creamy perfection to his hungry gaze. Her breasts were full rose-tipped orbs that beckoned for his touch, her waist was narrow, her belly flat and her legs lean and muscular, but Rutger felt his eyes pulled irresistibly back up their shapely length to the triangular nest of black silken curls. A flash of modesty, and he felt the flutter of her hands attempting to cover herself, but he caught her wrists easily, and kissed her until she was writhing beneath him with wanting. The friction against him was maddening, and Rutger lifted himself, wanting the torture to last—still refusing to think past the feel of her body against his.

Still gently holding her wrists with one hand, Rutger caressed one breast, lightly circling its warmth until he leaned over to capture its stiff peak in his mouth, letting his tongue graze over the sensitive crest back and forth until she arched against him with a soft cry. His free hand swept slowly lower tracing a path of fire until he found the moist heat between her legs. A maidenly instinct made her stiffen but he soothed her with kisses and gently began moving against her until she relaxed under his hands. With tender fingers, he stimulated the velvet core of her pleasure, and gradually increased the tempo of his strokes, matching his movements to the reactions of her body against him. At last, he sensed the wall of ecstasy overtake her as she melted in his hands, crying out his name as the spasms of rapture made her buck wildly in his arms. He released her hands, holding her as the last of the euphoria eddied through her lithe frame.

Blind Aphrodite

He embraced her as she returned to herself, savoring the gift of her climax, even as his own body clamored for a similar release. She smiled up at him contentedly, and Rutger closed his eyes to try to seize this instant for all time. Her hands reached up to frame his face, smoothing over his uneven cheeks, and Rutger's eyes started open in shock. Ice exploded in his chest and he was free of her touch and standing by the bed in seconds.

"Rutger?" Claire sat up, pulling the blankets to her chest modestly, her voice threaded with fear and uncertainty at his sudden abandonment.

He was speechless, still trying to understand what had just happened. She hadn't flinched, or looked startled, and a part of him began praying to every god it could think of that he had simply moved too quickly for her to realize what her touch had encountered. On its heels came fear and regret and a thousand other feelings unrecognized.

"Is it because I'm blind?"

He almost said no, but looked up at the ivory creature that occupied his bed—a fantasy vision that he had achieved at too great a personal price. Hopelessness overwhelmed him, and the ogre in him howled in defense, "Yes! It's because you're blind!"

The words struck her like a blow, and something in him died at the sight of it. "No," she whispered, empty eyes seeking to meet his.

"Yes," his whisper was like knife in his own heart, "That's why I can't go on with this. I took advantage of you. It's a lie, Claire, and the fates are too cruel to allow me to steal my happiness by destroying any chance for your own." He turned away, unable to look any longer at her stricken face. "You wouldn't be in my bed if you weren't blind." Hysterical laughter bubbled up from the well of pain in his stomach.

"Stop this," she pleaded, her voice breaking against him like a whip.

"I will stop this. The irony is killing me! If you could see, I could no more touch you than touch the moon—and I'm the villain for trespassing knowing that. Villain and Fool, at your service, madam," he was unable to stop himself from making a courtly bow with the last brutal words.

"How dare you!" the anger in her voice made him straighten quickly, the shift from quiet hurt catching him off guard. "What are you saying, Captain?" She stood to face him, wrapping the blanket around her. "That I can't love you because I can't see your face? Because I don't know that you're scarred?"

"No," there was no air behind the word, and he doubted she even heard it in her fury.

"How *dare* you! You think I'm some shallow creature that I wouldn't have seen past it? Well, I see past it now. You're selfish, and—and—blind! *You're* the one who is blind! Blind to anyone's pain but your own. Blind to anything but your own fear. I thought you would understand what it was like—" She faltered for only an instant, then recovered from the fury that choked her. "Leave me alone!"

She moved away from him with hands outstretched towards her room.

"Claire, wait!" he reached out to stop her, but she must have sensed him and shifted to avoid his hands.

"Don't touch me!" Her voice dropped to a venomous growl, "You are the monster you fear, and I am the fool for believing otherwise." With that she retreated to her chamber, and slammed the door.

She had been icy Diana in the moonlight, wild and powerful, wrapped like a Grecian beauty in her makeshift sheath, one bared shoulder completing the picture. Fury had made her eyes sparkle like black opals, and Rutger experienced pain like no other.

Omigod, I love her. The unmistakable sound of the steel bolt sliding home was like a hammer blow and he knew he had lost.

*   *   *

Claire's composure shattered as she locked her door for the first time and threw herself down onto the bunk, hot tears burning her eyes as she sobbed uncontrollably. Of course she knew he was scarred! There had

Blind Aphrodite

been dozens of subtle signals, especially from his protective crew. But it had been Samson's story that had given her the last clues to his pain. Samson had said that Rutger had been blown to hell and back and had lost himself in the aftermath of that battle. Her instincts had filled in the rest. But she had been sure that she could reach him. She had meant to tell him all the wonderful speeches she had practiced waiting for him. But when he had cried out in his dreams, she had gone to him without words and lost herself in his touch. She had given herself to him completely, positive that her acceptance and love had been evident in every instant, confident that there would be time enough later to talk about their fears and the wonderful future that awaited them.

But he had made it clear that he had seen nothing but her sightlessness. She was just a blind pawn that he regretted toying with, but couldn't credit as his equal. She was to be pitied, a helpless creature he had lied to and manipulated, and hated himself for hurting. Weakness—it was the only quality he had recognized.

She cursed herself for the naïve fantasies that had made her believe him to be any different from the rest of the world. Like Olivia and all the others, he considered her someone he could control for his own purposes. She had thought herself in love, recklessly throwing herself into his arms, only to discover that he hadn't wanted her love. He had been attracted to her because she was blind and he could use her to feel like himself again. He had wanted to play at some rogue's farce in which she had simply been a willing participant. If his own conscience stung him for it, she was glad.

Her tears began to slow, and she moved to curl up on the window seat to lean her warm forehead against the soothing cool panes. He was wrong to have thought her weak, she told herself. Claire determined to set aside her foolish dreams of a knight in shining armor. It was a trap that had led her into his selfish, wicked arms. She wouldn't let herself give another moment of thought to Captain Rutger Grayson. It was Edward she would think of now—only Edward.

Chapter Ten

Philip watched the claret in his crystal glass rock with the motion of the *Hermes*, and did his best to ignore the spike of pain in his skull along with the droning wheezes of his host. Captain Whitburton was exactly the sort of man that Philip usually went to great lengths to avoid—dim-witted and pretentious, ill mannered and boring. The Captain prided himself on having exquisite taste in art and had subjected Philip ad nauseum to his clever stories on how he acquired his collections. As Philip glanced up from his glass to see Whitburton push yet another piece of cake into his mouth before continuing his tale of a quest for nautical masterpieces, he decided he had received enough punishment for one evening.

"I am sorry to interrupt this fascinating story," he said regretfully coming to his feet. "But I find myself fatigued this evening."

"Not up for our usual game of cards, Lord Forthglade?" Captain Whitburton almost pouted in disappointment, looking like a fat child denied a favorite outing.

The spike in Philip's head seemed to twist at the sight. "Tomorrow night, you have my word. Good evening, Captain Whitburton." He left the dining room without another word, reaching his spacious cabin before he realized that he was still holding the glass of claret in his hand. He smiled at the evidence of his obvious haste to escape his host's good company.

The cramped confines of the *Hermes* wreaked havoc on his nerves and Philip wondered how men survived the hellish prison of ocean voyages.

Blind Aphrodite

He missed his valet and servants as he set his glass down to begin untying his cravat and dark blue silk solitaire. He had necessarily traveled without entourage, a rich prize motivating him to speed and sacrifice. He wondered if it may have been a mistake to bring Olivia, but he did not regret her presence entirely.

Not entirely, he thought as a wicked smile crossed his lips. She had not been pleased with her confinement aboard ship, and had finally overcome her initial bout of seasickness. Philip's mouth pulled into a taut line as he picked up his glass again. Sickness, of any kind, disgusted him and he had made it clear that he had no patience for this weakness. But she had apparently recovered, and then proven to him that she was ready for any rigorous activities he cared to pursue. He knew she had anticipated a voyage with ready physical access to him, but Philip found the notion boring and dangerous. He much preferred to keep his secrets, fighting the demons that lurked in briny shadows.

She chafed under her role as a glorified servant he was bringing to attend his new colonial bride upon their return to England. He had introduced her as a prim widow, and then proceeded to primarily ignore her in the presence of the crew. He loved the way she bristled when he ordered her about in front of Whitburton. Almost in answer to his thoughts, he heard her soft knock on his door.

Olivia came in without waiting for his response, impatient to talk to him. "I thought you were going to include me for dinner at the Captain's table this evening."

Widow black flattered her blond coloring, and Philip noted that his 'prim' widow had the lush body of a courtesan. But her tone made him frown as his headache reasserted its presence behind his eyes. "I spared you the tedium, tigress. Be grateful to have missed the experience." He tossed the remaining claret down his throat, hoping it would numb his pain. "Now, I am in no mood for complaints from my housekeeper on—"

"I am *not* your housekeeper!" she hissed, taking a step forward as if to battle him physically.

His eyes narrowed dangerously and she halted her advance. "Of course you aren't. But neither have I introduced you as my mistress, so pardon me for attempting to be playful, tigress. If you wish to have dinner with the Captain, I am sure it can be arranged. It might draw unwanted attention to the fact that you are unfashionably beautiful for a chaperone, but I suppose you are clever enough to address that issue." His voice was clipped and dry, causing her to shiver.

She seemed to reconsider her approach, dropping her chin to give him a seductive look through her long lashes. "Unfashionably beautiful did you say?"

"You're lucky I let you leave your cabin at all," an icy smile answered her efforts. "You should see the eyes of the men as you pass them."

"They look at me, do they?" she was playing the coquette for him now.

"Imagine if they knew what a tigress you can be. Imagine if they knew that under that bonnet is a woman without shame. Imagine if they knew I would pay to watch them have you." His headache was gone in a flash of black cruelty and he felt the first hint of excitement as the color drained from her face.

Olivia froze, the teasing pout still on her lips. He often said things to shock her, but something in his eyes made her heart skip a beat. She knew enough about her lover to know that to show real fear would be to lose face with him, even though his words made her want to scream in protest. He wouldn't dare—would he? Philip's behavior had been increasingly difficult to anticipate as the days at sea wore on. Fear had become a new element in the relationship that she considered herself too clever to ignore. She had no choice but to call his bluff, forcing her face into a mask of indifference. "Shall I call for the quarter master? He seems a likely candidate."

Blind Aphrodite

"Perhaps, later." He reached out a hand and then pulled her roughly towards the bed. Later, as she lay satiated if somewhat bruised beside him while he slept; Olivia pondered the dangerous nature of her partnership with Lord Forthglade. Asleep, he was a dark Adonis, the picture of a perfect gentleman with noble features and a well-formed body. But her Adonis had a taste for unconventional love, and ignited within her the most forbidden desires. Initially, her lust had kept pace with his. But lately, she began to feel as if the path had no resolution, only becoming more treacherous and perverted. She wanted him even now, but Philip's love play was turning threatening. For now, she sensed the presence of a restless boredom in him that frightened her more than anything else could. His words were never without meaning, and Olivia knew that any sensual fantasy of his making could potentially become reality.

No matter the cost, she accepted that she would submit to any sinister sexual game he desired. She had come too far down the twisted path. It was too late to turn back now or plead for an awakening modesty. She would do anything in order to keep him at her side. At least until Claire's fortunes were in their hands, and then—Olivia comforted herself, if it came down to it, the first newlywed Lady Forthglade might not be the last tragic death in their little drama.

Chapter Eleven

The crew of the *RavenSong* did their best not to interfere in the strange truce that seemed to exist between the Captain and his Lady. Samson's dire predictions of how they'd spend the rest of the voyage at opposite ends of the ship had proven wrong. It was as if Rutger had met his match when it came to stubborn natures and the ability to deny a hurt. The breakfasts continued, with both of them in attendance. Neither one addressing the other, or only with the greatest politeness. Samson took over the walks, and learned quickly not to ask about the fateful night of his disastrous matchmaking mission. Instead Lady Claire talked about her brother and all his travels. Samson told her about some of the places that the *RavenSong* had rested her bow, careful to skirt any stories of her more questionable adventures. Dinners had also become communal, although most of the officers begged off, unwilling to face the pain in the Captain's eyes as he followed her every gesture. Only Cutter was a mainstay, apparently suffering from guilt at having been an accomplice in the previous deception duped by his smooth talking first mate.

At last the *RavenSong* drew into port, and Claire's heart lurched at the sounds of the men preparing to make landfall. Finally, she could find the truth about Edward and begin to search for him in earnest. But the thought of leaving the *RavenSong* and saying goodbye to its crew filled her with dread. Except the Captain, of course. Claire's resolve to despise him had begun to fade, as his attentions never seemed to waver. His every

Blind Aphrodite

kindness was a stone against the wall she had put up against him. Her determination to set him from her heart had been a dismal failure, but the gulf between them was insurmountable. After all, Claire told herself with a firm set of her chin, 'I will always be blind.' So, she had tried to ignore him for the remainder of the voyage, and he had borne it with patience. They never spoke of what had happened in his cabin that night, even as Claire habitually bolted her door against him.

Claire moved her hands across the stiff leather spines of his library, secretly wishing that she had had more time to hear more of these treasures read in Rutger's expressive male tones. A knock at the door, and Claire called for the expected Mr. Cutter to come in with a promised tonic for her melancholy.

"Pardon, Miss Aylesbury," Rutger's voice made her step away from the shelves like a guilty child. "Mr. Cutter sent this small vial with his compliments, as I insisted on making the delivery myself."

He had returned to using her formal address, and Claire felt its weight on her already dampened mood. "Thank you, Captain Grayson. Please just set it on the table. I'm afraid I'm not aware why it required your personal attention."

"We will be at the Savannah docks in just a few hours, Miss Aylesbury. I thought we should discuss our plans." The distance of his voice across the room let her know that he remained just inside the doorway. "We should have spoken of this before, but it never seemed an appropriate time."

"*Our* plans?" Claire answered in shock, "*My* plans involve hiring a guide and then looking for my brother. I will compensate you for my passage and your trouble and then *you* will be free to go as you wish."

"I wish to honor our original agreement."

"Our original agreement was that you would bring me to Savannah. You have fulfilled your end of the contract." Claire began to feel a wariness overtake her at the calm energy that seemed to flow from where he stood.

She moved to the window seat to retrieve her pouch, and reached inside to hold out her mother's necklace, its cold stones lying heavily across her fingers. "Here, payment for dispensing your duty."

"I recall it differently."

"And what exactly, Captain Grayson, is your recollection?"

"That I would bring you to Savannah and help you look for your brother." His voice was firm and unyielding.

Claire was speechless until she recovered to dispute him. "But after—I would never expect you to—"

"If you believe nothing else about me, Miss Aylesbury, believe that I am a man of my word. You said it meant your life to find your brother, Edward. You asked for my help, and I pledged to give it."

"But I don't want your help!" the words were defiant, but even as she spoke them Claire felt their untruth ring in her ears like cheap tin.

"I beg your forgiveness, but I find it difficult to believe that you are looking forward to searching in a strange city in a strange land that is even now in the middle of a rebellious dispute against the crown. The town is teeming with soldiers, rebels and dangerous traitors. You would be a woman alone in—"

"You mean a *blind* woman alone, don't you, Captain?" she hated the lump that rose in her throat as she faced him.

He continued without hesitation, "—in a port town without any connections to speak of. Edward may not even still be in Savannah, and if your investigation leads you closer to the fighting, you will need reliable passage and protection. Rail all you wish, Miss Aylesbury, but I would no sooner abandon you here than I would at the frozen north without shoes. Besides, even if I would consider it," she could hear the cynical smile in his voice now, "the men would mutiny before I'd barely ordered the first line dropped, and then you would be exactly where you started—with help."

Even as another argument rose to her lips, Claire felt the logic of his stance hold her in place. If London had seemed overwhelming, then

Blind Aphrodite

Savannah could only be exponentially more frightening as the great unknown. She knew no one in the colonies, and had not really thought about how her 'search' might unfold in reality. She needed him, now more than ever. It was a revelation that made her want to scream with frustration, her fingers closing on diamonds that burned with the heat of her shame.

"We will reunite you with your brother, and then, you can render payment if you still wish it."

"Very well, Captain Grayson," she relented, her back stiff with anger, "I shall rely on you and your men to assist me. But I cannot stay aboard the ship after we dock. It is simply too—"

"Ah, yes," he finished her thought as she struggled for the right words. "The proximity has become troublesome." Silence hung in the air between them until Rutger continued, "I will arrange for respectable and safe accommodations in town."

"Thank you, Captain Grayson."

"You are welcome, Miss Aylesbury." And he left her to her thoughts.

*   *   *

Once docked, Samson joined Rutger in the ship's hold going over their trade goods. "Pardon the interruption, Captain," he began genially, "But I wanted to ask if I should stop anywhere to ask about Lord Aylesbury on my way back from the charter house."

"Don't bother, Samson. I'll check in with the harbor master myself, and also make sure the local military leadership is 'barely aware' of our presence. We can't afford to be commissioned until we assist Miss Aylesbury, and even then, my first inclination is to leave them to their pointless squabbles."

Samson sputtered at this unheard of change in routine. "But you never leave the Song if—"

"Assign one of the officers to keep Lady Claire occupied and off the decks for now. Tell Cutter to locate the very best boarding he can with house servants for Miss Aylesbury and also to arrange for a more complete wardrobe. She cannot continue to make due with only four dresses. Spare no expense, and tell him no pastels."

"No pastels," Samson echoed in dull shock, as if discussing a lady's wardrobe were as normal as the weather.

"Arrange for the dressmaker to come to Miss Aylesbury's new accommodations as soon as she's settled. In the meantime, help Mallory get this cargo off-loaded and make sure we aren't cheated of a farthing. Have Sweet remind the men to keep their shore leave close to hand and to go only in-groups of four. I don't want to lose anyone or to have any trouble while we're here. Tell everyone that it's low profile and absolutely *no* politics. I'll get Miss Aylesbury moved and settled when I return, so tell Cutter to get moving on a suitable inn."

"You're serious," Samson asked, a grin breaking over his face.

"Of course, I'm serious, you old badger," he growled back, "And what in God's name is so funny?"

"Just pleased to see you acting like your old self again, Rutger, my friend."

"That's Muck to you, old friend." Rutger's smile lit his eyes and he knew that Samson was right.

Samson's face sobered suddenly, "What happens if we don't find him?"

Rutger hesitated, the darkest possibilities crowding his thoughts and cutting off his words. At last he recovered, "We'll find him easily enough. Lord Aylesbury's trail will be simple to find—a young, handsome, wealthy English Lord travelling in style. He won't have gone unnoticed, even in the colonies, or rather, *especially* in the colonies. He's probably just gotten sidetracked on some foolishness and forgotten to write. If it's anything else—there will be time enough to decide what to do next. Until then, she's still my responsibility. Whether she likes it or not."

Blind Aphrodite

Samson left him to his inventory and to carry out Muck's orders. Samson only prayed that Rutger was right and that they would all be able to put this latest chapter of heartache behind them soon.

* * *

From the start, their search had seemed stalled and hopeless. For all of Rutger's professed optimism, he had begun to doubt if Edward had ever reached Savannah. After settling Claire into the Garden Street Inn, they had searched in earnest for contacts in the port town that might remember meeting Lord Aylesbury or have a notion as to his current whereabouts. Using Edward's last letter as a vague guide, they followed every clue for over a week and a half to dead ends and empty houses. Claire had insisted on being actively involved with the search, accompanying Mr. Cutter or Samson as they made inquiries. The rebellion worked against them. Every one seemed suspicious and unwilling to converse with strangers, and Rutger was sure that his bizarre appearance wasn't helping.

Still, he refused to give up. Claire's courageous spirit drove him on. He wondered if she were aware of the changes in him. He walked with his head held high, ignoring the usual reactions of the locals. A wardrobe long locked away had been aired out, and Rutger deliberately chose from his better coats for their excursions. Colors and fabrics made to flatter and purchased in youthful vanity were dusted off to once again see the light of day. To help Claire, he had forced himself to overcome his shame. In the days since she had locked her heart against him, he had accepted the loss of his fantasies in exchange for the realities of an impossible love. Rutger had no thought of winning her back, but was determined to restore Claire's trust and his own sense of honor. To achieve both, he had to find a way to provide for her happiness. It seemed that the only way to make her happy would be to find Edward and then let her go. He couldn't see beyond that moment, and could only hope honor alone would sustain him later.

"Another pint, governor?" the barmaid's offer cut into dark thoughts and a darker mood. Rutger glanced up to nod acceptance, noting the girl's fresh appearance and buxom curves. As she poured the ale, he was startled to catch her flirting wink. "Not planning on drinking alone, are you?"

"I'm expecting a friend," he tried to keep the surprise out of his voice, "Kind of you to ask, miss."

She smiled, shifting the weight of the large pitcher to one hip and moved away to the next table. Rutger ignored the feelings that stirred with the simple exchange, and glanced again towards the open door of the Red Wolf Tavern. Like countless other taverns and ale-houses the world over, the Red Wolf seemed to have its share of private corners and open benches for the locals to occupy for both business and pleasure. He had chosen the Wolf as a place to meet yet another would-be informant for its accessibility and reputation for nondiscrimination against scoundrels of every flavor. Currency and free-commerce were the Red Wolf's only requirements, suiting his purpose perfectly. In over a week's searching, he had tried to establish a reputation for being extremely generous when it came to the tiniest piece of information about Lord Aylesbury. He could only hope that his funds would begin to generate results soon.

Rutger spotted his contact the instant he entered the room. The clerk from one of the local trading houses looked as if he would jump out of his own skin at the first loud noise. He was thin, with hawk-like features that made him look terribly nervous and fierce at the same time. Rutger signaled from his private table, and was relieved that his 'friend' didn't faint at the sight.

As Mr. Lorring edged into his seat, Rutger did his best to reassure him, "Thank you for coming, sir. May I buy you a pint for your trouble?"

"Yes, th-that would be fine," his eyes darted about the room, avoiding Rutger's face.

Blind Aphrodite

Rutger caught the eye of the wench easily, and then decided not to waste any time for fear his 'informant' would bolt for the door at the first opportunity. "I am looking for Lord Aylesbury, a dear friend. He came to Savannah almost six months ago, but has not been heard from since."

"And wh-what makes you think that I would know anything about this?" Lorring's bird-like face was set defensively, but Rutger recognized the opening for bidding.

"I understand you have a good vantage point on the comings and goings of this town. Your family is well-connected to local society, and you might have heard of a well-to-do English gentleman arriving unexpectedly in these, shall we say, 'unsettled' times?" as he spoke, Rutger lay several coins across the table in front of him to underline his points.

The money captured Mr. Lorring's attention completely. "You are a friend of this gentleman's?"

"A dear friend," Rutger echoed quietly. "I am simply concerned for his safety."

"And if I assist you, then my name is forgotten?"

"I confess, I've forgotten it already." Rutger sat as still as he could, waiting for the tide to turn.

"Times are uncertain, and a man doesn't wish to lose friends while enemies abound." The high-strung clerk spoke to himself, talking through his own fears in the familiar warmth of the Wolf's hearth. "You've been seen all about the docks, so none could say that I was the man to point you towards Sir Brewster, could they?"

"Towards who?" the gentle question was laced with intensity.

The coins began disappearing off the table one by one into the clerk's pockets as he spoke. "I myself don't move in the finest circles, but if any nobility came to town, they would at one time or another pay respects to Sir Basil Brewster. He knows everyone and is always anxious to make acquaintances with anyone from back home."

"Homesick, is he?"

"A patriot, sir." Mr. Lorring's tone was defensive, and then he paled as if he had said too much for only a few pounds sterling.

"Yes, a patriot. As are we all," he stood to leave Mr. Lorring to his tankard and to the friendly attentions of the wench now headed back towards the table. He tipped his hat courteously to her as he passed, and then tried to contain his own enthusiasm for the first break in their search. Instinct told him that this was a real lead, but practical caution urged him not to get too excited. The last thing he wanted was to disappoint Claire—yet again.

Chapter Twelve

∽

"Almost done, miss." The maid gave the corset one more tug, and Claire did her best not to make an unladylike protest. After just a few weeks of freedom aboard the *RavenSong*, Claire discovered that she had not grown nostalgic about fashion in that time. Out of necessity, she had abandoned confining corsets since there had been no one to lace her at sea. The bodice was confining to say the least, and now with the weight of her farthingale and petticoats, she wondered how she had ever managed to move about wearing so many layers.

"Arms up for the dress now, miss." Bess' instructions were well practiced and kind. Claire obliged by raising her arms as Bess dropped the morning dress over her head. Despite her temporary discomfort, Claire couldn't help but admire the soft whispering sound of the fabric and the soft feel of it as it swept around her. As Bess laced the dress, she smoothed her hands over the texture of the embroidered silk with its matching patterned brocade underskirt. At last, Bess turned her about for a final inspection, ignoring the high color in her blind mistress' face.

"The colors suit you, Miss Claire. 'Tis the green of it that brings out your eyes and the purple is just the right touch."

Claire smiled at the image that came to her, "I don't look like a peacock, or a bunch of grapes?"

"Hush, now!" Bess sounded mortified. "You're a beauty, and a lucky creature to have a Lord with such good taste. Every color he chose suits you perfect—"

"Bess!" Claire's patience was at an end, "For the last time, you will not presume so much! Captain Grayson is simply escorting me to the colonies to locate my brother. He is not 'my lord'. And besides," she added with a stamp of her foot, "It was Mr. Clive, the dressmaker, who chose the fabrics."

"As you say, miss, as you say." Bess was completely unruffled, enjoying her mistress' show of spirit. The maids of the inn were all quite taken with their blind guest, but also with the romance of a rugged sea captain clearly besotted. True, his scars were daunting, but even little Molly the youngest scullery maid agreed that he was like a man out of a fairy story with his gold eyes and hair. Bess knew for a fact that the Captain had intercepted the dressmaker and chosen the colors and combinations that would befit Miss Aylesbury. Mr. Clive's creative pride had been soothed with coins, and he had been sworn to secrecy—the maids however, were under no such oath.

Claire bristled at Bess' casual attitude, but decided it was a battle not worth the effort. Any mention of the Captain made her feel unsettled, and Claire tried changing the subject to avoid the clamor of her own heart. "Mr. Cutter should be here any moment, Bess. Please help me find my walking stick and gloves, won't you?"

As Bess moved to find the requested items and handed them to Claire, there was a soft knock at the door. "Come in, Mr. Cutter," Claire called and then continued at the sound of the door opening and a man's steps, "As you can see, I am ready on schedule for once. Bess assures me I don't look like grapes, but her description has left me a little unsure."

Rutger's laughter made her stop in her tracks, and Claire felt warm heat flood her cheeks at its unexpected sound and the flutter of feelings it set off beneath her tight laces. A rich sound, like dark honey, and Claire

Blind Aphrodite

wanted to laugh and cry at the forgotten melody of his pleasure. It had been several days since they had met to talk about their search and the lack of progress. Long days and longer nights and Claire had congratulated herself on how well she was doing to focus only on Edward and not to give treacherous Capt. Grayson a second thought.

"Miss Aylesbury, of all the descriptions and comparisons, I'm afraid 'grapes' wouldn't make the roughest list." His manner was courtly, but Claire purposefully ignored his implied compliments.

"Captain Grayson, you certainly enjoy surprising me. No great feat, of course, considering my handicap, but in the future, I would appreciate it if you would announce yourself before arriving uninvited." Claire drew her shoulders up in chilled indignation, striking out to regain her inner-balance.

Bess' shocked gasp told her that the tactic wasn't completely ineffective, but Rutger's response was friendly and even. "I apologize for catching you off guard, Miss Aylesbury. It was only in my haste to bring you the latest news on our search that I omitted—"

"News?" anger was forgotten instantly, and Claire cut him off quickly. "Is it Edward?"

"A new lead, but a promising one. I thought we should go together for our best chance at success."

"Yes, of course." The word 'together' echoed in her ears, but Claire forced herself to concentrate on the issue at hand. "What sort of lead is it?"

"A local gentleman who prides himself on his social connections. Your title will gain us admittance, and if he doesn't respond to beauty, perhaps I could play the beast." His tone was light, but Claire reached out without realizing it to touch his hand in an eternal gesture of comfort.

"Rutger, don't—"

He moved away from her touch, stopping her words. "I have hired a carriage. I'll wait for you downstairs, Miss Aylesbury."

Renee Bernard

Silence swarmed the room as the door closed behind him. Claire felt her knees wobble until a stern voice in her head reminded her how well she was doing without the odious man and his selfish games.

"Oh my!" Bess interjected, "Besotted like idiots, the both of you! What a world!" And she began hustling a stunned Claire out the door. Claire allowed her maid's cheeky assistance down the stairs, unable to protest Bess' interpretation of events. Claire knew that Bess was wrong, but let her repeated protests die on her lips. "What a world, indeed."

When at last she emerged into the late morning sunshine, Rutger felt his breath catch at the sight. He couldn't lie to himself and say that he had forgotten how lovely Claire was. Rutger knew that the image of her was indelibly marked in his memory. The jade green of the dress was dazzling, and set off her hair and eyes perfectly. Bess had somehow tamed Claire's wild curls into a lovely arrangement of waves capped with a matching green bonnet with lavender ribbons. Her stunning curves were set off by the simplicity of the dress, and Mr. Clive had followed his instructions to the letter when it came to the materials and cut. The wide farthingale accented a tiny waist, and the modesty of the gown did nothing to dampen her startling appeal. It had been a dangerous indulgence, the last of his fantasies turning against him. What had started out as an innocent gesture to help her feel more settled, had become subtle torture as he realized the inappropriateness of dressing a woman he had no claim to. Without intending it, he had placed another lie between them. Knowing that she hated him and would never have allowed it, he had arranged it quietly and then instructed Mr. Cutter to give her the impression that expenses were being added to his 'compensation'.

It occurred to Rutger that Claire was essentially correct in her judgement of his character. He had been selfish. Even in defeat, he found himself taking every opportunity to be with her. Ignoring her feelings,

Blind Aphrodite

he chose the honorable path for his own salvation, but also because he knew the truth of his feelings and was determined to have her in sight as long as possible.

It was his feelings for Claire that wrestled him to speechless wonder every time he saw her. His attachment was profound, and seemed to deepen every hour that he lived with it. Her sympathetic touch moments before had been a brand against his skin. He had thought the scars were a living hell, but a future without Claire redefined the word 'suffering'. Resignation warred with wasted hope, and Rutger forced himself to concentrate on the 'honorable' course ahead of him.

* * *

The carriage ride to Sir Brewster's townhouse was mercifully brief, and Claire did her best to focus on thoughts of her brother and his recovery. Sounds of the port city through the carriage's open windows made it easier to disregard the powerful male presence sitting across from her. Rutger had finished telling her about their lead, and Claire could do little to contain her nerves. If the informant was accurate, then meeting a local dignitary like Basil Brewster sounded like something Edward would have done without fail. Edward was an idealist, but he had a streak of the practical as well. Many of his letters described local citizens and British expatriates he had met on his journeys. Why would he change his habits in Savannah? Claire didn't realize she was fidgeting, until the carriage stopped and she noticed that she was still in agitated motion.

"Don't worry, Miss Aylesbury." His voice was soft and reassuring in the small space. "Just think of it as a simple social call to pay our respects. We'll learn everything we need to, as soon as we're meant to."

Claire gave him her bravest smile and tried to absorb the calm, confidence of his tone.

"Just follow my lead," he dropped his voice conspiratorially, and Claire's smile relaxed at the picture of what unlikely spies they would make.

Whatever lead Rutger had planned was overwhelmed at the unexpected greeting they received. Rutger had no sooner knocked on the entryway and asked if Sir Brewster were receiving callers, when a friendly storm seemed to sweep them into the house.

"What is it, Jonah?" Claire heard an archly British voice asking only to have the speaker decide he was too impatient to wait out his servant's reply. "Never mind, as I am not home to—Heavens! It cannot be!"

"Sir Brewster?" Rutger was doing his best to try to regain control.

"It's Miss Aylesbury, or I am not Basil Brewster!" A now jovial, and distinctly less arch voice came near, and Claire found her hands being taken for a very enthusiastic greeting and then pulled through the doorway. "You are the spitting image of your brother, bless you! Did Edward recommend you to call? What a pleasant surprise!"

Claire couldn't help but smile at Brewster's effusiveness, but also at the joy of hearing him mention Edward in the present tense. Unfortunately, she didn't seem to be able to get a word in edgewise, and their host had yet to release her hands as he continued to pull her deeper into the house. Sir Basil Brewster was a short man and Claire had the impression of a round man as well, from the feel of his chubby fingers and his gait. His breath rattled a bit in his chest, and the smell of the paste in his hair combined with a hint of snuff rounded out Claire's image of the man. She could hear and feel Rutger behind her, and wondered how he was reacting to the commotion.

"I am Miss Aylesbury and Edward is—" she began to no avail.

"Edward is a naughty young Earl and a delightful young man," Sir Brewster laughed, "What a stir and how many Savannah belles has he sent to their rooms in tears! In my younger days, I'd have given him a run for— oh my! I don't believe I know this ferocious looking gentleman."

Blind Aphrodite

"Captain Rutger Grayson, at your service, sir." Rutger's voice was deeper than usual, and Claire recognized his displeasure. "We are most anxious to find Miss Aylesbury's brother, and had hoped that you would—"

"Come and sit down then, come and sit." Sir Brewster proved incapable of letting anyone finish their sentences, "Jonah, bring tea for my guests."

Claire winced as her shin met with a low table, and at last, managed to free her hands from Sir Basil's surprised grasp even as she heard Rutger's soft growl at their host's ignorance. "Tea would be lovely, Sir Brewster. Perhaps you could continue about Ed—"

"Bless you, you're blind!" He was the soul of sympathy, and began to 'assist her' to her chair. "I had no idea, my dear. You looked right at me as if you could see. What an amazing trick! Edward never mentioned it, not even once when he described you. What a terrible sibling to omit such a detail!"

His kind prodding to steer Claire onto the nearest chair was apparently more than Rutger could bear to witness. "Sir Basil, Miss Aylesbury can seat herself! She is not an invalid, I can assure you, and is far too well mannered to ask you to contain your misdirected attention. I on the other hand, have no such restrictions." He had stepped closer to intervene, and Claire held up a hand to stop him.

"Captain, please!" Claire knew he meant well, but she couldn't risk offending someone who might know of Edward's whereabouts. "I apologize, Sir Brewster. It's just that we are anxious for news of my brother, and I'm afraid the search has frustrated us both beyond reason."

Sir Brewster was flustered, but recovered quickly. "No apologies necessary. My attentions were sincere, and it is clear the Captain looks out for your best interests." His mood seemed to lift as they all were finally seated in his bright formal room. "Now, let us speak at last about your brother. I'm afraid I grew quite fond of him. What a dashing young man!"

"When did you see him?" Claire couldn't stop the question, or the dozen others that clamored for answers. "Where is he now, do you know? Did he tell you where he might be headed next? Or can you—"

"Oh my! I see you are indeed in a state, my dear. And no wonder! I will offer what small comforts I can, but I'm afraid I am as anxious as you are about our Lord Aylesbury." Sir Basil took a deep wet breath, and Claire forced herself to be still while he gathered his thoughts. "Your brother is quite a cutting figure, I remember him vividly even though it has been some months since he called. He had graciously accepted an invitation to stay for a few days, and I had been planning a small reception for Savannah society to introduce him. The troubles have robbed us of so many happy occasions, it seemed like a great boon to have an excuse for a party." He paused here, as if waiting for some agreement from his captive audience.

Claire obliged her mouth dry with fear. "How very thoughtful of you. Edward loved parties."

"Well, he has a distressing way of showing it, my dear! Imagine how worried I was when he simply left the day before the party to go into town and then, poof! He never returned! Without so much as a by your leave, and good-bye! What could I do? I searched and inquired, but no one had seen my guest and I know everyone in Savannah worth asking!"

"He—vanished?" Claire whispered, not sure what she had expected him to say.

"Frankly, I was stumped," Sir Brewster exhaled a loud sigh. "Left his trunk! I'll have it brought to you of course. Fearless, young man. No doubt he met with foul play to leave his things behind. An impressment gang could have taken him. He could be on some ship headed towards the Indies doing rough labor. Or perhaps he decided to have some sport on the docks in one of the alehouses. In times like these, unrest abounds and the darker elements would have been glad to rob and attack a well-to-do English gentleman."

Blind Aphrodite

"Sir Brewster, I think that's enough—" Rutger tried to break in to end his dire musings.

"Quite the card player, your brother. Men are murdered over games of chance oft times. Although, I checked with the authorities for any signs of a corpse, and none had been reported. Of course, in Savannah it would be all too easy to just toss a weighted body into the river, or the ocean itself."

Claire had listened to Brewster's list of horrors with a growing sense of disconnection. His voice grew more and more distant and hollow, and Claire allowed that perhaps if the room would stop spinning, she would insist that Sir Basil were mistaken. Grey mist intermingled with the white streaks of light from the windows, and then a roaring sound overtook Brewster and there was nothingness.

Claire awoke to find herself lying along what could only be a satin covered fainting couch. A rush of embarrassment and misery flooded her cheeks, and she fought the nausea that threatened to overwhelm her. It was Rutger's hand that held hers tightly, and she clung to it as if to draw from his strength.

"You fainted, my dear!" Sir Brewster announced from the foot of the couch sounding at once anxious for her but pleased with his uncanny diagnosis.

"Nonsense, Sir Brewster!" Claire answered, pushing herself up from the cushions. "I never faint." Tears filled her eyes, and Claire was sure that she was the most undignified and wretched woman on the earth.

"Take a moment to recover, Claire," Rutger's voice was low and meant only for her ears as he shifted to shield her from Sir Basil's nervous hovering. "There's no shame in this."

Claire lifted her eyes to his face, the white glare from the windows outlining his head and shoulders. Even as a darkened blur, he stirred her with his broad shoulders and firm lines. She pleaded with him silently, unable to speak past the lump in her throat. 'Take me from this place, Rutger. I don't want to hear any more. I *can't* hear any more.'

Without turning from her, he answered her pleas and spoke directly to Brewster. "I am taking her back to the Inn. Miss Aylesbury has had enough for one day."

"Oh, but she could stay here! I have elegant guest rooms, and I would be honored to—"

Claire gave him one firm shake of her head, and Rutger was deaf to Brewster's pleas. "We will call again soon. Thank you for your hospitality, but Miss Aylesbury will be far more comfortable in her own rooms." He swept her off the couch, and to the shocked gasps and sputters of his host, proceeded towards the door. "Can you walk, Claire?" he whispered.

"Yes, I believe so." At that, he lowered her gently to her feet, letting go only when he seemed assured of her balance.

"Here is your cane, and now just lean against my arm." He spoke as if this were the most natural exit one could make, even as Sir Basil caught up with them to make one last effort to stop them.

"I cannot let you leave in such a state, Miss Aylesbury! I am sure that Captain Grayson presumes too much for your health—"

It was Claire who cut him off as tears fell unheeded down her pale cheeks. "He presumes nothing! Captain Grayson has been only too considerate in his actions. Now, if you will excuse me, I must return to my search. Good day, Sir Brewster." A tiny pull on Rutger's arm and he guided her gently down the steps and up into their waiting carriage.

It was in the confines of the carriage that she gave in to despair, crying shamelessly against the soft velvet of Rutger's coat. Images of Edward murdered and floating at the bottom of a watery grave haunted her and she clung to Rutger as sobs wrung through her frame. His arms came around her and he silently held her until her cries settled into tiny hiccups.

"Oh god! I've been so foolish." Claire lamented. "What did I expect? That he would greet us at the door and Edward would be behind him?" She hated herself for being so weak in front of him, but it took too much energy to be brave.

Blind Aphrodite

"I blame myself for getting your hopes up, when I could just as easily have gone to see him without you. I just thought he had such a reputation for pretentious—"

"Not everything is your fault, Captain," Claire stopped him, "It could just as easily have been the break we were hoping for. I'm the one who has dragged you into this stupid chase when we both know that Edward is probably—" She couldn't finish the thought aloud, as if saying it would seal Edward's fate. Tears flowed again, and any argument he could offer was stopped by her sorrow.

He held her until the carriage pulled up to the Garden Street Inn, and then he gently helped her alight onto the walkway. They stood for a moment alone, as Bess awaited them on the steps to help Miss Aylesbury up to her rooms. Claire was grateful for the pause that allowed her to regain at least a fragile shell of composure before facing Bess' friendly banter.

"It isn't over, Claire," he had dropped the formal address without realizing it, and Claire smiled at the sound of it on his lips. They had traveled so far together, and even now, she wondered how it was possible to care for someone so deeply and to feel so terribly alone.

"It isn't over," he repeated the words, his voice was clear and strong. But Claire knew that saying something wasn't a talisman powerful enough to make it a reality.

"Perhaps," it was the best reply she could make, and Bess came to take her arm to lead her weary charge inside.

*   *   *

"Another taste, darling?" Olivia leaned forward in the swaying carriage, offering another strawberry from the lunch basket she had packed. Philip had been on his best behavior ever since their arrival in Savannah, and now sat across from her at complete ease with himself.

"Not hungry, then?" Olivia began to withdraw her hand only to watch the picture of male relaxation evaporating before her eyes into a hunter's alertness. She slowly raised the plump berry to her lips and traced its sweet contours with her tongue, all the while watching in fascination the effects of her sensual spell. Just as he began to lean forward across the small space, she bit down decisively and coldly ended the teasing play. "Suit yourself, Lord Forthglade."

He relaxed against the padded bench, enjoying his tigress' games. It was late in the afternoon, and they were coming back from an impromptu picnic at his cousin's country estate. He had pushed her too far in the oppressive confines of their voyage from England, and Philip had made a conscious effort to reassure Olivia of his 'honorable' intentions. She was essential to his plans and he had no guarantee of controlling Claire without her assistance. But at the thought of their helpless quarry, he couldn't help but grin at how beautifully his schemes were coming together.

"You look supremely confident, dearest heart," Olivia's mood matched his. "For a man who seems content to let his 'fiancée' gad about town endlessly in the company of common sailors."

"I'm simply allowing her time to come to terms with the loss of her only brother, and to expend enough energy on her pointless quest to satisfy her own conscience."

"And to break her spirit?" Olivia added coldly.

"If necessary," Philip turned to watch the view, his thoughts considering entertainments for the evening ahead. "She's getting nowhere, and her champion is a complete loss."

"Are you sure? Captain Grayson didn't strike me as a fool." Olivia almost spat out the hated name.

"My contact at the Red Wolf has been keeping a close eye on him for me. Grayson meets idiots who tell him nothing for his money."

Blind Aphrodite

"I thought you meant for her to find him. Isn't that why you arranged to see Edward the day we arrived?" Olivia pressed, a pout coming to her lips at his inattentiveness.

Philip returned his focus to his petulant companion. For all her cleverness, Philip wished she didn't insist on him outlining what he considered obvious points. Although he realized at her expression, that her insistence had little to do with Claire and more to do with a desire for attention. "We win either way, my tigress. If she never finds him, it is all the simpler for us. We rescue her from her own grief, and she falls into my comforting arms. Even with Edward primed by us, it is still risky to rely on him to unknowingly assist our cause. Human beings have a way of exercising free will, sweetness." At the last, he pounded on the top of the carriage and bellowed orders to the driver, "Another tour around town, my good man."

"Philip," Olivia whispered, "Shouldn't you be more discreet?"

"I'm simply hungry, tigress. And you should know better than to tease." Olivia did know better, and moved towards him to demonstrate just how she wished the game to be played. In the dim interior of the carriage, Philip allowed her to take her pleasure as they moved through the crowded streets.

*   *   *

When they arrived back at the Lion's Gate Inn, Olivia rang for a bath and settled into their room while Philip drank downstairs in the common room. After the maids emptied the last of their steaming buckets of water, they left her to enjoy her private luxuries. She leaned back and closed her eyes, replaying the events of the day. Picnics and lusty carriage rides—exactly what her life would be once she became Lady Forthglade. She decided that she had finally recovered from the terrible voyage to Savannah. Weeks of seasickness had taken their toll, and Philip's dark games on board the *Hermes* still haunted her dreams. Strangely, she knew that there were gaps in her memory of their journey. She suspected that Philip may have hurt her somehow, but her mind had erected a barrier against it now. Olivia sat up in the water to apply oil to her skin with trembling fingers, mentally pushing away from thoughts of what may have passed between them on the ship. It was in the past, and she had more pressing matters in her present and future.

While Philip seemed content to await Claire's endless search and enjoy the chase, Olivia felt a different urgency. She knew that she was carrying Philip's child. While there were still some weeks yet before her body betrayed her secret, Olivia was determined to put herself in Claire's path as quickly as possible. She would discover the truth of Claire's progress and start the wheel moving towards Claire's marriage and demise.

She rinsed and stood to step carefully from the canvas-lined tub and wrap herself in a soft robe. She sat on the bed and began brushing out her long, long blonde tresses. Olivia was more determined than ever to achieve her true place in the world. She was the true Lady Forthglade and the mother of Philip's heir. Philip loved her completely. She was sure of it. All they lacked was the fortune that would ensure a comfortable future for them both. Once Claire's money was in their hands, she would tell Philip about the baby. Her hand slowed its strokes as a flutter of fear escaped the confines of her control. His reaction to her illness on board the *Hermes* had been one of complete disgust. She prayed he would view the inconveniences of pregnancy with more understanding. She had once considered destroying Philip if he betrayed her, but now being with child, it was as if an invisible hand closed on her throat. The barrier in her mind seemed to shake and she knew that time was running out.

Chapter Thirteen

◯

Rutger stood outside the Inn's gate, staring at the door that had closed behind Claire and left him to his thoughts. The late afternoon sun cast a glow on the street scene, but Rutger saw none of its beauty. Claire's pain had wounded him to the quick, and Rutger wondered how much more of this search could he inflict on her before giving up and somehow letting her go. She had seemed so sure of her brother's well being when they set out, but now he couldn't believe that Edward was still alive. False confidence faded quickly and Rutger realized he had never considered what the next step would be if Edward were dead.

Had he secretly wished for it? Was his soul so black that he could want her to be alone in the world and in need of his 'protection'? A sound of disgust escaped him, and Rutger turned from the gate to head back towards the carriage only to nearly stumble into a passerby who had paused next to him.

"Excuse me, sir!" Rutger was amazed at his lack of alertness. In another place and time, the oversight could have meant his end.

"I'm right fine, sir." He was dressed in a craftsman's garment, young enough to be an apprentice, but by his bearing Rutger guessed he was a freeman. "That was John Bunting's sister, wasn't it?" The stranger's question made time seemed to hold its breath, and Rutger halted in his tracks.

"The lady from the carriage?" Rutger asked evenly.

"Just so!" the man seemed pleased at making the connection.

"What makes you say this?" Rutger fought to keep his mind's clamoring questions from his eyes.

"Why she is his spitting image, and John is a man I'm not likely to forget!" The man's smile dissipated and his expression grew more guarded. "You'll pardon me, sir." He began to move away.

"Wait!" Rutger hoped he didn't seem too desperate. "I'm Captain Rutger Grayson of the *RavenSong*." He held out his hand in greeting, unsure of how to keep this man talking or if what he was saying was just a case of mistaken identity.

"Are you a friend, sir?"

"Yes." Rutger's outstretched hand never wavered, and at last, the gesture was answered with a warm grip and a shake.

"I'm known as Clay," the man introduced himself. "It's a bit of a joke since I'm a potter."

"Can I buy you a drink, friend?" Rutger felt relief but also a new anxiety at this unexpected turn of events.

"Just so! The Bell Tavern is just down this road, and the service is fine enough for patriots."

Rutger dismissed the carriage and driver, and they walked the short distance to the Bell. He didn't press for information, but allowed the friendly Clay to relax over a pint before inviting him to share what he knew of John Bunting. "It is welcome to meet someone who knows John."

"It was a shame, my friend. A true shame," the words were sorrowful, and Rutger felt his stomach flip at the pronouncement. And then Clay continued, "It was his first meeting, I'm sure of it. I was glad to meet him and introduce him to the others, and when the speeches began, you never saw a man more taken with patriotic zeal. His questions were just so, and he impressed more than a few with his resolve and manners."

"He is a good man." Rutger held his breath at the unbelievable tale of Edward's fate.

Blind Aphrodite

"When the redcoats came, it was chaos and while they normally try to capture our leaders and speakers, they seemed to head straight for poor John. That's when I knew he must have been working independently to support our cause, and they had laid a trap for him. The meetings are always dangerous, but are we not free men to gather and express our opinions? Has the crown and parliament lost all sense of morality that her colonists are no better than slaves to serve her without individual rights?"

Rutger held up a hand to try to quiet his friend's patriotic speech, but also to try to quiet his own inner storms. Edward and John Bunting, if they were the same man, then Edward was a condemned traitor. Death in a dockside fight was beginning to sound like a happier alternative. "When was this meeting?"

"Months since, in December if I remember it right enough." Clay tipped back his tankard, and then returned to his tale. "Yes, just so, December. That was how he mentioned a sister. We spoke before the meeting, and he said he missed her at this time of year. Considering a return home, but felt drawn to the cause and wanted to learn more."

"What happened to him?" For a moment the world seemed to hang on the answer, and Rutger wished he could take it back.

"A fate I wouldn't wish on the Devil himself. British prison ship, the *Laconia*." Clay returned in sad quiet to his ale, letting Rutger absorb the news.

A prison ship was floating death, and Rutger closed his eyes against the memories of his only visit to a British hold. Another time, another place and he had sworn to stay clear of the damn things for all eternity. "In port here?" his voice was raw in his throat, and he hoped Clay hadn't noticed.

"Just so." Clay nodded, "You can see her in the harbor, and when the wind is right you swear you can smell it."

"I should be getting back to my own ship, Clay." Rutger left coins on the table above the cost of the two tankards.

Clay's hand stopped him, "No need for payment, friend. Tell me, is his sister well married then?"

"Pardon?" Rutger asked in confusion.

"John didn't seem like a wealthy ne'er-do-well, but his sister seemed a cut above. Did she marry well?" Clay looked hopeful, but his curiosity might also hide a barb of suspicion about Rutger's own business in Savannah.

"Just so." Rutger left him at the table, feeling several pairs of eyes track his retreat. The Bell was no place for a man with Rutger's history and he was only too aware of how dangerous the search had just become. The sun was just beginning to set, and Rutger walked slowly taking a different route back towards the ship, while he considered his options. Clay could be wrong about 'John Bunting', and Rutger knew he could never risk exposing Claire to what might only be a painful theory. After her reaction to Brewster, he decided that it would be better to leave her out of this matter until he was sure. It would be safer to call on the prison ship tomorrow, at first light, but Rutger was unable to wait. It was too preposterous that a titled Earl and English Lord would allow himself to be mixed up in some treasonous meeting regarding a fight that was none of his concern. It was too incredible!

But everything was wasted speculation until he made his way onto the *Laconia*. Safer to wait, but Rutger decided that nothing would stop him from paying a call on Mr. John Bunting—not even the nightmare of a prison ship and the personal demons that screamed in his ears at the thought of setting one foot on its decks. Another time, another place, he reminded himself. For Claire's sake he picked up his pace while he prepared to pay a social call on hell.

* * *

It was full dark by the time his skiff pulled alongside the Laconia. He ignored Samson and Mallory's scowls and neither one of them spoke to

Blind Aphrodite

their friend while they rowed. The stench from the ship pinched their expressions into grimaces, while Muck sat in the bow seemingly unaffected. In the last few weeks, they seemed to have accepted Muck's moments of insanity. Samson gave Mallory a look that said he only hoped to survive this one.

"Halt! Who goes there?" The lanterns on the ship gave the musket muzzles a dull shine, and Rutger stood to hail the uniformed guards, determined not to show any fear.

He raised his own lantern high; lighting his face and letting them look their fill of his twisted features. "I am Captain Rutger Grayson, of the RavenSong. I've papers to verify my position, and have come to make an urgent call on one of your prisoners. Permission to come aboard?"

Seconds stretched out, and Rutger began to consider that he may have come just this far and no farther, when the rope ladder uncoiled down the ship's side. "Just yourself, Captain!"

Samson began to protest, but Rutger handed him the lantern and made his way up the swaying ladder too quickly for argument.

Once on the slick decks, he faced the guards as if it were the most ordinary occurrence in the world to face loaded muskets and request to call on a prisoner of war after nightfall. He withdrew his paperwork slowly from an inside coat pocket, keeping an unconcerned expression on his face as the men instinctively tightened their hold on their weapons. He passed the papers over to the more senior ranked of the two, and then leaned against the rail while they deciphered its meaning, startled by a royal seal and signature.

"On the king's business then, Captain?" the guard asked, his voice tinged with awe, eyes avoiding the left side of his face.

Rutger turned to give him a chilling look of iced bronze, "Most assuredly, sir. But its exact nature is not open to discussion. Let the

Shipmaster know I wish to see John Bunting, if he hasn't rotted to death on this barge."

No one moved, and Rutger pushed away from the rail to stand to his full height. "Unless you've found my charter not in order?" He extended a hand for the return of his papers.

"No—no, everything seems authentic. It's just that the Commander is off ship at the moment, and I'm under orders not to deviate from routine while he's out."

"I see," Rutger glared his displeasure, but then decided to try another tactic. "You are both to be commended for your dedication to duty. But I can only imagine how displeased your Commander would be to know that you refused to assist me. Gentleman, only the hour of this visit deviates from your routine, and I would not have chosen the hour if it weren't extremely urgent that I see John Bunting tonight. If you prefer not to report the visit to your Commander, I would understand. But you rob me of the opportunity to praise you when I meet with him tomorrow."

"Of course, I suppose we can make an exception in your case, but please don't mention it to the Commander." They both looked embarrassed, and Rutger eased their minds considerably as a small pouch of coins changed hands. "Right this way, Captain. Mind your footing."

Rutger's legs felt wooden as he followed the guard into the dark bowels of the ship. He kept his eyes on the back of the man's head, desperate to ignore the nightmare images that bore into his peripheral vision. The smell was beyond description as men lay in their own filth and rats feasted on the weak and dying. Rutger's prayers for the mysterious Mr. Bunting to be on the first deck went unanswered and he found himself at least two levels down into the nightmare, before the guard began reaching for his keys.

"Try to keep it quiet, Captain, or you'll have the whole ship howling before you know it."

Blind Aphrodite

"I'll do my best," he whispered, fighting down the bile that seemed to rise in his throat as the foul air filled his mouth when he spoke. The guard had unlocked the iron-slatted door, and it swung back with a rusty squeal that ignored the request for quiet. A single occupant was silhouetted against the corner, no windows for ventilation, and a pile of molding straw on the floor and a rusting bucket in the corner for 'necessities'. Rutger wondered how a human being could maintain their sanity in such a place. But then, a dark demon whispered from the past, *you know the answer to that, don't you, Muck?*

"Five minutes, Captain, and then I'll retrieve you." The guard handed him the lantern and moved to lock the door behind him.

"Is that all the time I'm allowed?" Rutger asked, surprised at how indignant he managed to sound.

"Never known anyone to want to stay down here more than five, Captain." At that the door closed, and Rutger's knees shook at the sound of the bolt lock sliding into place. If the guard's suspicions got the better of them, or they decided to betray him, he and John Bunting could share a final fate.

The prisoner sat in the corner; filthy and blinking like a mole under the lantern's glow. Rutger felt his own terror melt at the sight of a familiar face in this place. His hair was ebony, and even in lanky strings, he recognized its color and curl. The eyes that squinted to adjust to the light were the color of the ocean before a storm and the masculine cast of features did nothing to hide his resemblance to Claire. Rutger had no doubt that Clay would have made the connection between the two so easily. Claire had said he was her 'twin soul' and his appearance made the reasons clear.

'John' struggled to his feet, and Rutger realized that starvation had given him the illusion of being Claire's height and size, but her brother was nearly as tall as Rutger. Despite the rags, he held himself with dignity, and Rutger had to admire his calm demeanor.

"Lord Edward Aylesbury, the Fourth Earl of Clarence, I presume?" If Rutger had expected shock or gratitude, he was to be disappointed. His question met with no reaction, only an unblinking blue-green stare. "I see, perhaps I'm mistaken. The resemblance is striking after all."

Silence rang in Rutger's ears in reply and he fought the urge to shake Claire's stubborn counterpart until his teeth rattled. "Captain Rutger Grayson, at your service. We've come a long way to find you, but I'm afraid I never expected to find you here." Rutger felt precious seconds slipping away, and decided there was no time for shy games. "Your sister will be overjoyed to discover that you're alive, although I'm not sure she'll be pleased by your choice of accommodations."

"She—she's here? I can't believe it." The voice was hoarse from lack of use, or endless screaming. Rutger knew it could be either one.

"In Savannah. I thought your sister one of the most stubborn people I'd ever met, but you're making me rethink my ranking system."

"Who are you exactly, and how is it that my sister is here with someone like you?" he bit off the words as if they were distasteful, and Rutger bristled at the question.

"I am no one of consequence, your Lordship. Just someone trying to help—"

"Don't call me that! It's John Bunting. Do you hear me? If my identity is revealed you destroy everything that's left to her! Or is that why you're here? Blackmail, is it?"

"Blackmail?" Rutger tried not to smile but couldn't prevent it. Unfortunately, to Edward's unpracticed eyes the expression had the look of demonic confirmation.

"So be it, but as you can see, I am hardly in a position to negotiate, Grayson, so get on with your threats."

"You're an idiot, John Bunting. The only threat to your sister is having a selfish and politically stupid man for a brother. I'm not the one who

Blind Aphrodite

endangers her by going off on some foolish 'world tour' leaving my blind sister alone to fend for herself against fortune hunters and ogres."

"How dare you! My politics and personal choices are—" Edward seemed to suddenly lose his train of thought and grow impossibly paler. "What did you say about Claire being blind?"

The use of her name confirmed Edward's identity in Rutger's mind, but his shock at the obvious fact set him back on his heels. "It's true. That's why she couldn't search for you alone."

"When? How?" All of his anger was gone, and Edward searched Rutger's eyes for the answers he didn't want to hear.

"Two years or more. From a fever, I believe." Rutger winced at each word's impact on Edward's weak frame. "I don't know the details, but she is remarkably sound and unaffected by it."

"Oh god, I should have known." Edward sank back into the corner, "I felt as if something were wrong, but when I asked in my letters, she made no mention." An empty laugh echoed in the small room, "I should have known when she kept asking me to describe every detail, all the colors." He couldn't go on.

"Now what, John?" Rutger tried to pull him back to their present dilemma.

"Blind and she came all this way, with *you*?" Edward was refocusing, but on exactly the topics that Rutger didn't want to discuss. "What was that about ogres again?"

"Drop it, John. It's her future we're trying to salvage." Rutger's guilt made his reply edgy, and he forced himself to meet Edward's unwavering gaze, so like Claire's.

"Her future is none of your concern, Grayson." Edward struggled again to his feet.

"And whose concern is it then? You've certainly gone out of your way to make things difficult for her. Was it worth sacrificing her future so that you could hear some rousing speeches and commit foul treason?" Rutger lashed out, only too aware that his own feelings were clouding his judgement in this pointless argument.

"I've never sacrificed her future! It's her future I'm protecting as John Bunting in this hole." His rage was quiet and frightening. "No one will ever know the fate of Edward, and her fortunes and estates will be left intact for her dowry. If I survive my sentence, then I return and all is restored. If I die here in the dark, then she at least has a fortune and lands to comfort and provide for her."

"She doesn't want fortune and lands," Rutger countered, "She wants her brother by her side."

"She is provided for, and I'll see to it somehow that she is looked after and protected until—until this nightmare is over." Edward's solution sounded hollow to Rutger.

"You are in no position to protect anyone, including yourself." Rutger dropped his voice, as a moan began from the cell across the hall. "What will you tell her when she finds you here?"

"She won't 'find me here'. There are absolutely no women allowed aboard the ship, and only a demon like yourself would consider bringing Claire into this foul stench!" Edward hissed at his nemesis.

The word stung like a whip's lashing, and before Rutger could recover he heard the return of the guard. "Very well, then, John. I leave you to your hole and your 'personal choices'. May you rot in peace until we meet again."

They faced each other with icy glares until the guard opened the door, and Rutger passed through it without a backward glance. He fumed the entire climb towards the blessed fresh sea air. 'Spoiled, arrogant, selfish bastard!' Rutger had envisioned hundreds of first meetings with the mysterious and missing 'Edward', but none had involved exchanging insults in the hold of a prison barge. He had no intentions of bringing Claire onto the barge, but he also had no intentions of lying to her. Edward was

Blind Aphrodite

alive, and he knew that resources could be quietly brought to bear to improve his situation. The war complicated matters, but nothing was insurmountable—nothing except Edward's stubborn temper.

When he at last stood on deck, he asked his hosts bluntly, "Where can I find the Commander?"

They mumbled directions to the harbor administration office and Rutger impatiently made his way back down the ladder. "Gentleman, row." Samson and Mallory didn't need to be asked twice, and they pulled away quickly from the barge eager to make an escape. Rutger looked out to the lights of the city where Claire waited and prayed for news of her twin. He dreaded giving her that news more than he had dreaded the smell of disease and death aboard the *Laconia*. Edward was both lost and found, and no matter what happened, he was inevitably one step closer to being forced to let her go.

*   *   *

Edward clamped a hand over his own mouth to keep from screaming as the precious light retreated with Grayson. Anger poured through him, and Edward seized the emotion as a shield against the dark terrors that inhabited his cell. Thank god for Philip! His visit the week before had been a godsend, and Edward gritted his teeth in shame when he recalled how he had doubted Lord Forthglade's dire warnings about the treacherous Grayson who sought to destroy his family's future.

Philip had promised to have him transferred to the port's jail and Edward now allowed himself to hope. He had survived only for Claire, his every thought and dream focused on her happiness. He imagined the beauty she would have become in his absence, and had always pictured her safe and happy in England wearing a rainbow of fashions and breaking countless hearts. When Philip had arrived, Edward had felt an overwhelming sense of panic. He had been terrified of being exposed in his current situation, only to hear Philip beg forgiveness for risking that same exposure. He recalled the moment with startling clarity.

Lord Forthglade confessed that he was desperately in love with Claire and had in fact proposed marriage and just received their Uncle's blessing, only to discover her missing! She had been stolen away from friends and family by a demon by the name of Grayson. Grayson had apparently taken advantage of her fears for her twin's safety, and lured her into his scheming clutches. Philip had only been able to follow them by forcing Olivia to reveal Edward's plight, and he had again begged Edward's forgiveness for risking all for love. He had offered to try to see to Edward's comforts, and tried to reassure him that he intended to rescue Claire and restore her personal honor and their family's future. He had pledged to see her safely home and away before all was lost.

At the time, Edward had been unable to entirely accept Philip's story since it forced him to loosen his hold on his reasons for remaining sane and alive. If Claire were in danger, Edward knew he couldn't survive the endless night of prison.

And now, the demon had presented himself! Forthglade had warned him about Grayson's appearance, but it had been another reason he hadn't believed Philip's tale. Why would beautiful Claire fall under the spell of such a base sailor with a twisted face? It wasn't possible! Edward moaned as Philip's words rang all too true. He had awoken to face a monster, and the reality of his innocent sister in Grayson's treacherous hands. But one thread of hope remained, and Edward put his head in his hands and began to pray. Philip had come all this way to reclaim his love, and Edward prayed to every saint he could recall that Claire would be safe under Lord Forthglade's protective wing before too long. And that she wasn't really blind. It seemed too cruel that they should both spend their lives in darkness.

Chapter Fourteen

◯

After a restless night of pacing and worry, Rutger had at last made his way to the harbor administration office and met with the prison ship's commander at first light. Surrounded by the unmistakable uniforms of the British military, Rutger had for once been grateful for his face. The men seemed to treat him with an additional measure of respect, as if seeing the battle scars as a badge of honor. It made the interview with the commanding officer that much easier to achieve. He kept his story simple, he was a man in love and hoped to win a woman's heart by trying to ease her brother's suffering. A deprecating comment about his face added just the right authenticity, and Rutger eased a small pouch of coins across the table. It had been readily accepted, along with his proposal to move John Bunting to the port jail. The commander had even surprised him by offering to ensure that things happened quickly, making John Bunting available for a visit as early as the following afternoon.

Rutger left with his head aching from days of tension. He had expected his appeals to take most of the day, and stifled a sense of alarm at the first easy turn in this journey. "You're tired, Muck and just dreading the next errand." He reproved himself, startled to hear his voice in his ears. Samson had always chided that Rutger's habit of speaking his thoughts aloud was a sign of a madman, and for once, Rutger considered that his friend might just be right. Ever since his first glimpse of Claire, reason and logic had been beyond his grasp. His heart had ruled his head, and he wondered if his head had suffered for it. It was too late to worry now, and Rutger reluctantly turned his feet towards the Garden Street Inn where Claire waited for news. Rutger paid no attention to the young soldier that ran past him, unaware that he carried a message to another 'interested party' regarding John Bunting's new accommodations.

Claire listened with only half an ear to Molly's sweet chatter as she stood pretending to look out over the Inn's gardens. She tried to imagine Edward waiting for her among its green paths, but her heart froze in protest. She had once told Captain Grayson that she would know if Edward were dead, that her spirit would have felt it. It was early June and Claire's heart was filled with icy fear. Despite the morning's warmth, a chill came over her and she hugged her arms for comfort. Sir John Brewster had said nothing that her soul hadn't confirmed and she had struggled all night to accept the truth. Edward had been alive only in her dreams, and she had run towards the protective arms of a ghost.

A knock at the door, and Bess entered with her usual lilting scolds, "Molly, you'll talk yourself to sickness, child! Leave the mistress to receive her guest." Molly left with a giggle, and Claire turned from the window waiting to hear the rest of this mysterious announcement. "Say what you like of your Captain, but he's obedient to a fault, ain't he? Insisted I announce him proper before escorting him upstairs; how's that for manners?"

"He is not my—" but Claire realized she didn't have the energy to fight a hopeless battle with Bess' unflagging optimism. "Please bring him up, Bess."

"I will at once, mistress. Although, would you like me to help you pinch some color to your cheeks first? You look a pale shadow of yourself, even wearing your pinks, miss."

Blind Aphrodite

"Bess, please! Just bring him up!" At last Bess left to do her bidding, and Claire knew the confrontation had done its work to bring color to her cheeks. She dreaded this meeting, but could find no escape. A night of rehearsed speeches fled her head as she heard his knock and heard him enter the room.

"Captain Grayson?" Claire's voice was weighted with uncertainty, and she frowned at the awkward beginning.

"You were expecting another gentleman caller, Miss Aylesbury?" Rutger's gentle teasing made her smile. "The azalea and rose pinks suit you, but I'm afraid he won't find me a very attractive accessory to your ensemble."

"How is it that your flattery always manages to make me think of the most rakish courtier, and yet you keep trying to convince me that you know nothing of useless social skills?" she responded playfully.

"I never said I knew nothing of useless social skills," he countered, "I believe I said I no longer had need of them."

"Come sit, Captain," Claire guided him to the sitting area. "I have something I want to tell you."

"My news is far more important, Miss Aylesbury." Rutger took the small settee she had indicated, anxious to keep his tone cheerful. After all, for Claire, it was good if not the best of news. It was only for Rutger that it felt like a funeral announcement.

"No, I insist on telling you my news first." Claire squared her shoulders and plunged ahead with her announcement. "After a long night's deliberation, I have finally accepted that my search for Edward is over. It was my own stubborn wish for Edward's life that made this seem possible and my own fears of a future alone. I will acquire documentation regarding his disappearance and return home to face the consequences of my foolish flight to—"

"Edward is alive, Claire." Rutger's words rushed past her unheard at first.

"No," she shook her head slowly. "You heard what Sir Basil said about his likely fate."

"I found him last night, and I swear to you that Edward is alive."

Claire felt the full impact of his words and came to her feet. "Alive? Where? How? Where?"

Rutger moved to take her hands, trying to steady her for the rest of the news. "Claire, please let me finish. Whatever you do, try to remember that he is alive and well." Rutger guided her back onto her chair, and knelt beside her keeping her cold hands in the warm well of his own calloused fingers. A cynical voice mocked him by pointing out that he looked like a man proposing marriage, instead of fulfilling a last obligation and counting the hours until he's dismissed. "Your brother was apparently in the wrong place at the wrong time, and has been convicted of treason." Claire gasped, but held herself still as he continued. "He wisely gave a false name and has deceived the authorities into thinking him a local freeman. They sentenced him to three years. I found him aboard a prison barge in the harbor."

"A false name? Why?" Claire struggled to comprehend this incredible twist.

"To protect your family's titles and fortunes. If his treason were published under his true name, your family would forfeit everything to the crown and become outcasts. He was trying to protect you, Claire."

"A prison ship?" her eyes widened in horror at the thought of the terrible mortality rate on the death ships. Plague and fevers were common in their damp hulls, and few men who were sentenced to them lived to return to describe the torments of perpetual darkness and suffering.

"I have arranged for him to spend a few days in the port jail, a great improvement over the barge. They will let you see him tomorrow afternoon, and then Edward himself can reassure you and you can both determine your next course of action."

Blind Aphrodite

"I am to see Edward tomorrow?" Elation warred with shock and Claire knew it was only a matter of time before tears overwhelmed her.

"Claire Bunting is to see her brother John Bunting," Rutger advised, drinking in the play of emotions across her lovely features. "You must remember to call him John, or you endanger both your lives."

"I'm not sure what to say! I was convinced that Edward was lost, only to discover that my only family is restored to me!" The anticipated tears began to fall at last.

"I took the liberty of sending Mr. Cutter to attend him to make sure that his health is as sound as possible in light of his situation." Rutger's own voice dropped with rough emotion.

"How can I ever repay you, Captain?" she asked the question breathlessly, but its weight seemed to strike them both.

He stood and bowed over her fingers, "Your—your happiness is payment enough, Miss Aylesbury." He moved beyond her grasp suddenly awkward and uncertain, "I'll leave you to your thoughts and Samson and I will come by with the carriage for you tomorrow after lunch."

Before she could think to stop him, she heard the door to her chambers close behind him. Claire wondered if she were destined to cry every single time she saw Rutger, and struggled with tears of joy intermingled with a sadder sense that her life had just changed and not entirely for the better.

At a knock at the door, she did her best to compose her features, hoping against hope that it was Rutger. At Sir Basil Brewster's hail, her smile wavered but she recovered quickly. "Sir Brewster, what a surprise!"

"I have brought your dear brother's things, and my heartfelt apologies for my insensitive display yesterday." His words were a preamble to the sounds of Bess and Molly's efforts as they lugged what was apparently Edward's largest traveling case through her narrow door. "I confess I never even inspected the contents for clues! It seemed a dishonorable tactic, but now perhaps you'll find better news amidst his shirts."

Remembering what Rutger had said about Edward's identity, Claire only nodded in agreement. "No apologies are needed, Sir Brewster. Your concern for Edward was evident, and it was kind of you to deliver these items personally. But if you'll excuse me I'm not—"

"Edward was like a dear nephew to me! What a tragic loss," he wheezed from the climb up the stairs, and she knew Bess would be waiting for her to request refreshments, but Claire decided she had had enough of polite Savannah society to last her a lifetime.

"I am not feeling well, Sir Brewster. A headache only, but Bess will show you out." Claire then did her best 'Olivia' imitation. "I am touched by your thoughtfulness at returning my dead brother's trunk, but I can only regret that your kindness did not extend toward sending a letter regarding his disappearance. A shame you did not consider Edward's family when you were so terribly inconvenienced by his disappearance and the cancellation of your party."

For the first time in his life, Basil Brewster was struck speechless.

"Good day to you, Mr. Brewster." With one last elegant curtsey, she dismissed him like a schoolboy and then turned her attention to Edward's possessions as Bess led a still dumbstruck Sir Brewster out the door.

*   *   *

Rutger felt the day stretch out endlessly, and resisted the urge to return to the sanctuary of the *RavenSong*. There would be time enough for Neptune's hermit to spend hours of unbroken solitude in the empty years that yawned before him. As he walked the narrow streets, it occurred to him that the citizens seemed to have simply accepted him while he wasn't paying attention. Cries of shock or dismay were starkly absent, and he wondered how much of his exile was self-imposed. He had shied from human contact for so long convinced that the world held little but pain for him. But Rutger didn't want to question his choices.

Blind Aphrodite

It was too late to take any of them back, and Rutger shook his head to force his thoughts away from their soul-searching quest. It was too close to self-pity for his personal comfort, and Rutger made his way defiantly into the Red Wolf Tavern to escape the regrets that haunted him.

The tavern's interior was dim and cool in the early afternoon, a welcome change from the bright heat of early summer. He made his way to the private booth he favored out of habit. As he sat down, he smiled at how quickly men create patterns that they can repeat for a sense of security. The barmaid's hail was equally familiar and Rutger greeted her with his best lop-sided grin. "May I trouble you for a tankard, my lady?"

Merry's face bloomed with a blushing smile that would have done any debutante credit. "For such sweet speech, I'd go to any trouble, sir." She brought him a full ale with her usual saunter, any trace of debutante lost in the open invitation in her eyes. Her gaze missed nothing, not his long shapely legs encased in soft fawn-colored leggings and high leather boots, or the trim of his matching coat and broad shoulders. She deliberately let her eyes linger on his face, marveling at his lion-like coloring and beautiful wrecked face.

It was a revelation to watch her approach, and Rutger accepted the tankard gratefully. "Thank you, Merry." Years ago, she would have been to his taste for tavern wenches. Red hair spilled from beneath her cap, and her complexion was rosy with health. Merry seemed to be well aware of her best assets, and flaunted her bounteous curves accordingly. Her temper was light, and Rutger had observed her quick steps about the room and easy humor. But as he studied her now, his brow furrowed at the lack of interest he felt. After years of frightened women, Merry should have been a welcome aberration. The insanity of instead only wanting a woman he could never have was profoundly depressing. In a day or two, Claire would come to realize that their mission was complete and he had no practical reason for lingering in a war side port with an empty cargo hold.

It was the ultimate folly to hang about when it looked like her twin-soul was about to reinforce every doubt she may have about Rutger's character. If their roles were altered and Claire was Rutger's sister, he knew he would order her to head home and steer clear of selfish ogres.

Merry leaned over to set down a board of bread and cheese in front of him, and Rutger was again treated to a knowing little wink. "Here to meet a friend again, governor?"

"Not likely, Merry. I've run out of friends today." Rutger forced himself to endure the flirtation, unwilling to accept the ruin of his heart for all time.

Her sympathetic pout was practiced, "How so? Is your search not going well?"

Something within him instinctively lied, "Not well at all. I believe I have had enough of chasing ghosts for one voyage." At least his melancholy was genuine.

"Poor thing," Merry settled against him, smelling of ale and warm bread. She placed a kiss on his left ear, making him stiffen at the gesture, "Come upstairs with me and I'll let you chase me all you wish."

He looked up into her face, hating the doubts that nibbled at his thoughts. "It is kind of you to offer, but you would be sadly disappointed with this particular hunter." He disengaged her as gently as he could and slipped a coin into her hands to soften the rejection. "A pretty girl should seek prettier company, Merry."

"A prettier man wouldn't be so kind," Merry answered with sad wisdom and left to tend other tables. Rutger finished his ale quickly, and fled the grip of loneliness that had settled around his heart. The *RavenSong* called and he made his way to her without looking back.

Chapter Fifteen

Sir Basil Brewster sat nervously fidgeting on the delicate chintz covered chair while his cousin paced the floor like a leopard. Philip had always made him nervous, and Basil was sure Philip took pleasure from this talent of intimidation.

Basil decided to end the uncomfortable silence, "I know that you—"

"You know nothing, Basil," Philip's reply was razor sharp. "And that is exactly why I tolerate and love you as I do. Beyond your own bellybutton, you are beautifully ignorant, cousin. Now, let's go over this again. Claire told you that she believes Edward dead?"

"Absolutely, Philip." His eyes followed Philip's every movement in morbid fascination, "Never seen a woman so upset and angry."

"Angry?" Philip wheeled about on the word, trying to match it to the glimpses of the woman he had met only briefly.

"That I hadn't sent word when he 'disappeared'. Cut me to the quick!" Basil supplied with a wounded squeak.

"Perfect." Philip slowed his pacing to consider his next steps. Basil had proven amazingly useful in his efforts to secure Claire's hand. When Olivia advised that Edward had written that he was making his way to Savannah, it had been a simple matter to send word to Basil about an eminent young man he should be sure to meet. Discovering Edward's propensity to treason had been a windfall, and under Philip's direction, Basil had made sure that Edward made the 'wrong' contacts to attend a rebel meeting. It was

Philip's idea to make sure that Basil suggested Edward leave his signet ring behind and use a false name in case of trouble. Sir Basil had then scored points with the local authorities by alerting them to a treasonous activity and had ensured that Edward would be taken. When Edward gave a false name, he played elegantly into their hands.

It might have been better if Edward had simply died aboard the barge, but Philip was glad to have a sound alternative plan for the moment. Claire had lost the trail and was now ripe for the picking. Once they were married, he would eliminate all his accomplices, including poor, unwitting Edward.

It was only Grayson that concerned him now. The man had shown himself to be tenacious, and his crew had proven above bribery when it came to information about their captain or his business in Savannah. He looked down at a still quivering Sir Brewster, sweat stains marking his expensive silk coat and a sauce stain from dinner marring his white cravat. He hid his distaste for his cousin's lack of control and wondered how they could in any way be related by blood.

"I have business to attend to, Basil," he gathered up his things in one fluid movement. "Keep to the house in the next few days, cousin, and I will come round to announce my engagement."

"Can we have a party to celebrate the news?" Basil sounded like a child begging for a pony.

"We'll see. My dear fiancée may not be in the mood for lavish balls considering her loss, but I will ask her when the time comes. Good enough?" Philip was in the mood to be benevolent, and even managed a courteous smile to Jonah on his way out the door. As he climbed into the closed carriage, he felt the first hint of a headache. He considered putting off his errand, but decided that timing might be critical if Claire were truly in the despair that Basil hinted at. He was sure he had already given her enough time to ease her conscience regarding a 'thorough search' for

Blind Aphrodite

Edward. Now he had only to ensure that Grayson had also abandoned hope, and the prize was his for the taking.

The Red Wolf Tavern was awash in activity as midnight drew near. Drunken song erupted without warning among the patrons who lost interest and quieted down before any second verse was reached. Merry kept her step lively to miss another rough pinch to her backside from one of her regulars. Another British regiment had arrived and word spread fast about the Red Wolf's ale and undiluted liquor. Of course, Merry liked to think that she had a little something to do with its popularity as well. 'Homesick boys, the lot of them,' she thought to herself, 'just looking forward to a friendly smile and a gentle touch.'

She scanned the room from behind the bar and caught sight of him immediately. In a room of swaying revelers, he was completely still in the entranceway. Just silhouetted against the night, she recognized him for the lines of his coat and his shapely silk hat. Dropping off tankards on the way, she met him quickly. "Coming in for a drink, governor? Or were you considering blocking my doorway all night?"

"Meet me in the stables," it was a command enforced by the gold piece he flashed in his palm. She reached for the coin, but he folded it away like a magician and repeated his condition, "The stables, Merry."

As busy as she was, the owner knew the wenches made extra coin as they chose and so she knew no one would question her absence for a few moments. She slipped out the back door and crossed the narrow lane towards the dimly lit stables. Philip was easy enough to find leaning against the last stall's divider.

She straightened her back to make sure her figure showed its best as she moved towards him with her best saunter. "I didn't expect you till tomorrow, my Lord."

Philip considered his jaded little informant in the stables flattering glow. He normally avoided whores finding no pleasure in their practiced perversions, but Merry retained a core of innocence despite her profession. He had paid her for information and not thought of extending their arrangement further—until now. "Come closer, Merry."

Merry eyed him warily, but took a few more steps to come face to face with her patron. She recognized the desire in his face, but hadn't necessarily expected it. This gentleman had made it clear what services he required for his coins. 'Of course,' she thought with a quiet smile, "Men often changed their minds.' She curtseyed slowly aware of the view it afforded him of her generous cleavage. "I am at your service, my Lord."

He smiled openly as Merry unwittingly imitated one of Olivia's best maneuvers. He felt himself stiffen with desire at the wicked irony of it, just as his headache settled into a quiet pulse. "I've that coin for you, Merry."

Like an eager child, she looked to his hands only to be disappointed at the lack of a gold flash in his palms. "Where?"

"Here," he whispered drawing her hand against his swollen length. "See if you can recover it in my pockets." Shock crossed her features, and Philip decided it was definitely worth a gold ducat to see that flutter of surprise and desire on her face. He held her wrist fast in his grip and with his eyes locked onto hers he began to show her exactly how the search should proceed. Merry's tongue ran over her lips nervously, and Philip gasped at the tiny gesture.

"Did you see our friend today, Merry?" his husky whisper made her shiver in the heat of the stable. His hand never stopped moving hers up and down his shaft, and Merry felt a strange heat of her own at the power throbbing beneath her fingers and the powerlessness of being in his grip.

"Yes," she replied and was rewarded as he pulled her against him, the motion of their hands now touching them both. She arched her hips against the sweet friction, only to gasp in shock when he forced her hand

Blind Aphrodite

to move against her own folds instead. She resisted him briefly, but couldn't escape his gaze or the strength of his hand controlling her own. Sensation began to override her protest, and she waited like an apt pupil for her master's next question.

"How goes his search, Merry?" he began to raise her skirt slowly no longer needing to press her against him as she willingly kept her place now.

"Poorly, my Lord." His hand cupped her bottom and then trailed around to take over the work of her fingers amidst the wet curls between her thighs. The captured hand was now held behind her back, arching her breasts against him. Merry had never known such torture and wondered if all fancy lords made love like a dark game. "He said he'd had enough of chasing—" the rest caught in her throat as his head dropped to moisten the thin cotton of her camisole over one rust-colored nipple.

"Of chasing?" he asked against her firm peak, and Merry thought she would die of pleasure from his breath against her sensitive crest while his fingers moved ever faster between her inner thighs.

"Ghosts!" she panted as her body began to find its own rhythm.

"Perfect," Philip raised his head and captured her eyes with his. "Now you'll earn the coin, Merry. If he comes again, you'll slip poison into his drink and the world will have one less freak." He had expected her to climax, but instead she stiffened and froze against him.

"No," it was the barest whisper, but Philip felt a spike of pain through his temple as if she had screamed in his face. He stopped instantly and released her roughly so that she stumbled deeper into the shadows of the stall.

His voice was patient and careful, as if explaining something to a child. "I will give you the poison, Merry. It will be completely undetectable and no harm will come to you. Grayson will have a heart attack, and you can even pretend to cry if that will make you feel better."

Merry felt completely off-balance at the sudden rejection, her body still throbbing with desire while a growing sense of alarm coursed through her. "I—I can't do it."

The spike twisted viciously and Philip closed his eyes for an instant to ward off the unspeakable pain she was causing him. His voice was icy calm, "Why not, Merry?"

"I—like him."

Something in him broke loose, and he lunged for her with the speed of a cobra. A black wave of pleasure overtook him when his hands closed around the whore's neck. He gave her no opportunity to scream or truly struggle, driving her head against the stable's brick wall again and again until the sound changed and his fingers were wet with blood.

He stood and washed his hands calmly in the water trough, marveling at how clear his head now felt. He made a quick sweep of his coat to ensure that he hadn't picked up any straw or debris during his little 'romp'. He even checked his pants pocket to reassure himself that he hadn't dropped his gold ducat. "Waste not, want not, Merry," he advised the lifeless girl lying hidden in the shadows. Lord Forthglade left the stables unnoticed and made his way down the alley back towards his own rooms and the eager and accommodating arms of his dearest Olivia.

Olivia nervously paced the room, one of her hands deep in a pocket twisting the parchment with the news of Edward's change of address. It had been several hours since Philip had left to see his cousin Sir Brewster, and she had begun to worry that Philip may have run into trouble. The private dinner she had ordered now sat congealing on the side table, the smell of it making her stomach rebel.

"Did you miss me, dearest?" Philip purred from the doorway making her start at his silent entrance.

Blind Aphrodite

"My god, Philip!" Olivia was breathless at his sudden appearance. "Where have you been? I've been half sick with worry."

He closed the door behind him, making no effort to disguise his impatience at her tone. "Don't act like an hysterical idiot, Olivia. I believe I have had enough of female dramatics for one evening."

"What does that mean?" she fought to keep her voice level, but felt a squeak of surprise escape her as he removed his cloak and she caught sight of blood on the cuffs of his sleeves. "What have you done, Philip?"

He located the source of her horrified stare quickly, then shrugged at the ruin of one of his favorite monogrammed silk shirts. "You ask too many questions. It is a habit you should consider altering, tigress."

Olivia took a deep breath, and tried to focus on their greater goal. "I apologize. It's just that I consider us partners. Don't you?"

His lips compressed into a thin line of displeasure that she recognized immediately. "I will do as I please, Olivia. At the moment, it pleases me to tell you nothing. In return, you will keep you beautiful mouth shut and do as you're told."

Nausea whipped through her frame at his cruel words. He hadn't spoken to her like that since their crossing. Some instinct warned her against showing him any fear. "Just tell me where you were, Philip."

"The Red Wolf." He moved to the sideboard to pour himself a glass of wine. "Merry tells me they've gotten nowhere." He finished the glass with one quick toss of his head and she watched some of the tension flow out of him.

At the mention of his source, Olivia recalled her own glad tidings. But before she told him, some part of her cried out for him to soothe the sting of his words. She forced a wooden smile to her lips. "Tell me you love me, Philip."

Dark storms brewed in his eyes as he set his glass down to face her. "Don't toy with me tonight, Olivia. I can assure you that I am in no mood."

Her eyes darted to the crimson stains on the lace at his wrists and she plunged ahead. "I'm afraid your informant is wrong, dearest. Now tell me again that you want me to be your wife. And that you love me." She was willing to risk anything for his assurance, desperate to hear his pledge.

He was completely still and then he answered softly, "Of course, I do." His brow furrowed and he raised his hand to his temple, rubbing his fingers for relief. "Now what makes you say the wench lied?"

Olivia took a step back at the gesture, new terror setting in at this sign of one of his infamous headaches. Her stomach protested again at the sight, but the smile never left her lips. "It looks like Capt. Ogre has arranged to move Edward to the portside jail for Claire's visit tomorrow. I'll manage to run into her to find out if your initial visit to her dear brother was successful, and to introduce your presence in port."

Philip's mouth dropped in shock, but recovered to give her one of his sweetest smiles. *I may need you after all, tigress*, he thought, letting the dark wave of pain subside. He started to undress slowly, letting his clothes fall in a pile on the floor.

His movements were smooth and seductive, and Olivia felt the dark magic of his eyes draw her in once more. He removed the shirt last, dropping it on top of the rest and then moved toward her completely unfettered by society's restraints. The naked lust in his eyes made her shiver and her memory faintly stirred as his eyes locked with hers.

"Tell me you love me, Philip." Her voice shook as he drew close, but he didn't seem to notice anything but his own desire to possess her in that moment.

"I love you." The words rang with ice, and Philip pushed her down onto the bed. Olivia expected him to undress her, but he pulled her skirts up and spread her naked thighs. Without any pretense of tenderness, he pushed her face away and held his hand over her head to keep her from looking at him, while he rammed his hardened sex into her again and

Blind Aphrodite

again. Olivia closed her eyes against the pain and pleasure of it, and then opened them only to see the bloody shirt in the middle of the floor. She couldn't take her eyes off of it as he rode her, pushing and grunting. Something in her wanted to cry and Olivia felt the force behind the wall in her mind begin to hammer and howl for escape.

Chapter Sixteen

The port jail was a two story stone structure, gray and daunting and Rutger had no doubt that to Edward's desperate eyes it was a palace compared to the barge. The ride to the jail had been an anxious one for them both. While Rutger was sure that Claire's thoughts were all for Edward now, he found himself trying to memorize each moment as one of the last where they would be alone together. She had worn the simple, wedgewood blue dress to play the part of John Bunting's sister. Rutger recalled that it was also the dress she was wearing the day he had shown her the secrets of the carvings and they had shared their first kiss. Unaware of his reverie, Claire clutched his arm oblivious in her nervous state of the pleasure she afforded him.

"Everything is going to be all right, Claire." He began haltingly, unsure of how to set her at ease when he felt like jumping out of his skin. Recklessly, he decided to take this last chance with her. "Claire, I hope that after everything that has happened, you can forgive me for—" The apology died on his lips. What could he say? Forgive me for loving you. Forgive me for wanting you. Forgive me for trying to take something that wasn't mine.

Soft, gloved fingertips reached up to gently touch his lips. "Only if you can forget what I said in anger. You have never been a monster to me, Captain. Never." And then she leaned over and kissed him. It was a chaste touch, powerful and sweet, and Rutger took only what she gave. The torment was heaven and he knew that this was likely his last taste of

Blind Aphrodite

real happiness. At last, she ended it, reluctantly letting him go as circumstances forced her. Her gloved hand now rested against his cheek.

Time had stood still and Rutger felt the sweetness of the moment fall away to the bitter truth that there was still nowhere for them to go. No escape from scars and blindness, titles and honor, and prisons—real and self-imposed.

The carriage stopped, and she pulled her fingers away. The moment had passed.

As Rutger helped her out of the carriage, he caught Samson's solemn gaze from his seat next to the driver. Without a word, Samson had understood the depths of Rutger's dilemma and come to offer his support

"Here's your basket now, Lady Claire," Samson passed down the wicker basket she had brought with a few of 'John's' belongings. "Be sure to tell John what a grand sailor you made, and be brave."

Claire looked up towards Samson's voice, relishing the familiar sound of his concern. "Thank you, Mr. Guilford. I shall certainly try." To her credit, her voice had only the smallest catch at the last, and her smile was sheer bravado as the basket passed to her hands.

"Allow me to carry it for you," Rutger offered.

"I need to hold it to keep my hands from shaking," Claire admitted She paused for a moment, her eyes dropping to the ground.

"What is it, Claire?" he asked quickly.

Her eyes sought his face, and Rutger's breath caught in his chest just as it had the first time he saw her in his quarters on the *RavenSong*. Blue-green crystal blazed up at him framed by black silken lashes and Rutger knew her impact on him would never lessen with the passage of time. "You are sure it is really 'John'?"

Her trust overwhelmed him. "I am sure." He cleared his throat softly before he could go on, "Come, Claire Bunting. I'm sure your brother is as anxious as you are. You shouldn't keep him waiting." He assisted her up the steps, out of habit giving her subtle clues about the path ahead and quietly describing the room as they entered.

The jailer was a squat bulldog of a man. He looked over Rutger's visitor's pass and official paperwork with cold derision, but signaled his reluctant approval with a terse nod. "I'll need to see the contents of the basket." He barked, and Claire meekly handed over the wicker handle for his inspection.

He pawed through it roughly, and began to protest the brandy bottle when Rutger succeeded in catching his eye. One raised eyebrow and the jailer apparently thought it not worth the trouble. "One visitor at a time! I'll not have a crowd to contend with."

"Oh!" Claire seemed surprised, and turned an anxious face towards Rutger.

Rutger had expected the condition, and gave Claire one last encouraging gentle squeeze of her elbow before allowing the guard to escort her to her brother. "Samson will wait with the carriage and he'll take you back whenever you're ready."

"You won't wait for me, Captain?" The question impaled him.

"I'm afraid I would only be in the way, Miss Bunting." He handed her the basket and watched the jailer lead her down the corridor to the prisoner's cells. He waited until the jailer returned to confirm that she was safe with John, before heading out to give Samson his instructions.

Claire's heart was pounding as the jailer led her to her brother's cell. She could smell whiskey, sweat and a hundred other odors she didn't care to define. Their steps echoed on the stone floors and walls, and Claire held her basket tightly reminding herself to be brave for Edward's sake. She had prayed for this meeting for so long that she felt numb with shock that it was actually going to happen.

"Sister to see you, John!" The jailer's sharp voice made her jump, "You've only a few minutes, so step lively." The sound of keys in a tumbler,

Blind Aphrodite

and then a hand at her back pushed her forward into what must be Edward's cell as the bars clanged shut behind her.

"Claire!" Edward's voice was choked with emotion and suddenly they were embracing and Claire felt the world fall into its proper place. Edward, her hero, her champion, her guardian, was alive! Millions of memories flooded through her, and she was laughing and crying at the same time.

"Let me see you!" Edward held her at arm's length, "Oh god! You're so beautiful! How could I have imagined you differently?"

"You imagined me differently?" she teased, falling into their old rhythm of sibling banter. "Was I to be fatter? Or did you just imagine me with warts astride a horse or something?"

He pulled her back into his embrace, "I don't care how beautiful you are, it's that wicked sense of humor that steals a brother's heart." It was as if he couldn't bear to let her go, and she felt the same. Long months of separation had done nothing to diminish their bond. Still holding her with his cheek resting against her hair he gritted his teeth against the pain of knowing that Claire had seen him like this. Above all, he had hoped to spare her all of this. But at least he now knew that Grayson had lied about her condition. She had looked straight into his eyes, and was perfectly sound.

In his arms, Claire began to take in the details of his thin frame and rough clothes. Finally she forced herself to push away from him, so that she could attend to practical matters. "I brought a basket with a few things, food and brandy, candles, writing supplies and a change of clothes. I dropped it at the cell door, I'm afraid, but I'm sure nothing's damaged." She moved away, and casually used her bamboo cane to seek out the basket, retrieving it easily. "Is there a table where we can set this?"

She turned back with a smile, only to find a strange silence in reply. "J-John?"

"How do you know that nothing is damaged?" The question was an odd whisper.

Claire held in place, sensing that this question was about more than baskets and brandy. "I didn't hear the glass break, and the smell of it would have intoxicated us both by now if it had."

"Tell me you're not blind, Claire."

Be brave, Samson's words came to her, and Claire lifted her chin defiantly.

"Tell me you're not blind," Edward asked again, the words solemn and measured.

"And if I were?" Claire answered in equally measured tones.

"You cannot be blind, Claire."

"Oh," she suddenly felt very small, "What a strange dilemma since I am quite blind. But if you prefer for me to lie, then I will say that I am not and you can be master of the universe again."

"Oh god," Edward's soft cry wrenched her heart. "What have I done?"

"You've done nothing!" Claire came forward to take his hands in hers. "Why must all the men in my life insist on taking all the blame? You leave nothing to sheer chance or fate! It was a fever. There was nothing you could have done to prevent it."

"Why didn't you tell me? I'd have come home instantly to be by your side and to take care of you!" Frustration made his voice rough, and she hated the pain she was causing him.

"That is exactly why I didn't send for you!" she took a breath to steady herself, determined to make him understand. "Your dreams mirrored mine, and it was my only chance to see the world—even if it was through your eyes. You wanted to explore before returning to England to fulfill obligations and duties. How could I love you as much as I do and deny you that freedom? You are my twin! Please don't hate me for trying to protect your freedom or for trying to find you to protect my own."

"I could never hate you, Claire." Edward led her to two wooden chairs and a table and they sat together. "It just worries me to think of you alone and helpless in the world."

Blind Aphrodite

"Do I seem helpless to you?" Claire felt indignation stain her cheeks, needing Edward of all people to appreciate her strengths.

"Not at the moment," he relented. "But you are so reckless, Claire! How can I survive this knowing that you have no one to turn to for protection?"

"I have you!" she pleaded, "Use your title and fortunes to get out of this mess and take me home!"

"No!" his voice was unyielding granite. "If I reveal my identity then we lose everything. I already feel like a coward for not standing up for my beliefs, but I found I couldn't sacrifice your future along with my own. That's why I sent word to Olivia to keep you safely in England and not to tell a soul what had happened. You were never to know—"

"Olivia!" Claire's shock was profound. "You were a part of the lies? You deliberately kept the truth from me? I thought you were dead! Do you know what that was like?"

"You *have* to forgive me," he stood from the table and began pacing in the confines of the small room. "I felt stripped of every choice! It was a dilemma similar to your own, Claire. If I told you, you would have insisted on coming here. The middle of a war is the last place I wanted you to be! Our family's fortunes are at stake. The sentence is only three years, and I'm strong and in good health. The risk was entirely mine, and win or lose, you would be spared."

Claire was dumbfounded at his speech. Betrayal and loss wrestled with the understanding of what it was like to face impossible choices. The years had changed them both apparently, and Claire felt her eyes fill with tears at her newest loss. Gone forever was a naïve perception of Edward as invincible and heroic. Even absorbing this grievous truth, Claire was unprepared for the next blow.

"I understand that Lord Forthglade has asked for your hand, and that our uncle has given his consent."

"What?" Claire felt as if she had been slapped. "How—"

He pulled her to her feet to face him as the sound of the jailer returning reached their ears, "Claire, please! It is the obvious solution to all our problems. Accepting his proposal secures your future, and with his influence my chances for survival increase."

"No!" Her protest was weak even in her own ears, as she fought against the endless and invisible conspiracy against her happiness.

"Consider it for my sake, if not for your own!" Edward persisted, "Please promise me that you will at least consider him. You must marry, Claire. Please."

Be brave. She reached up to hold his face in her hands, aching inside at what his pleas meant. "I will consider it, John. That is all I can promise you."

"Time's up!" the jailer's now familiar bark made them both jump.

"Claire," Edward pulled her close, "I know you'll make the right choice for us both."

She nodded, unable to respond through her tears. The jailer pulled them apart and escorted Claire from the room without any further chance for farewells. "You can visit again tomorrow afternoon, miss."

She did nothing to resist, a part of her grateful for the reprieve from Edward's painful request. She had convinced herself that Edward would be her salvation from a loveless match. She had never considered that Edward would be in agreement with Olivia, pressing her to consent to marry a man she hardly knew. Even worse, he was in trouble and had asked her to help save his life. The life of her twin hung in the balance and Claire was trapped at last.

Chapter Seventeen

⚭

Shopping for items for another care basket for Edward with Mr. Guilford was the best distraction for Claire. Samson was doing his best to cheer her, and had agreed to dismiss the carriage so that they could walk at their leisure. "Now, Lady Claire, a man cannot have too many stockings!"

Claire tried to smile, pushing away thoughts of Edward's life being reduced to its barest necessities while fighting for survival. It was less than two hours since she had left Edward's side, her thoughts and emotions in a storm of confusion. The changes in their fortunes in the last day were too great to comprehend for now. "I will leave the count to you, Samson, but promise me that there will still be room for soap and medicine."

"We'll leave nothing out!" Samson reassured her with a maternal pat on her arm as he guided her up the busy street. "Mu—Rutger made me a list, and there's none better at practical matters than the Captain."

"What did you call him?" Claire responded to the strange syllable, but also to the tension in Samson's touch.

"Rutger," the reply was firm and uncharacteristically short.

"Oh," Claire dropped the minor matter, familiar with Samson's ability to instantly withdraw if pressed. At Rutger's name, her own spirit quieted. In the midst of chaos, his kiss in the carriage had been like an oasis of peace and honesty. He had allowed her to control the moment, and the gift was not lost to her weary heart. While everyone else pushed or pulled, Rutger was the only one who let her take the lead. If only he—her next thought was lost as Samson halted his steps without warning, nearly causing her to trip.

"Ahoy!" Samson called out enthusiastically, waving his arm in a warm greeting. "What a surprise, Lady Claire! If I'm not mistaken, it's your dragon lady!"

Claire froze at this incredible turn. She had never confided in anyone but Rutger her fears of Olivia and Olivia's betrayal. "Samson! Wait!" she whispered, tugging at his arm desperate to avoid a confrontation on a public street.

It was too late. She was almost knocked off her feet in Olivia's emotional embrace, a cloud of expensive perfume enveloping them both. "Claire! Oh, thank God!" Olivia's voice was laced with tears. "You don't know what we've been through to find you! I've been worried to the point of illness, but never mind that now! Tell me that you are well and sound."

"I—I am well and sound," the answer was rote as Claire struggled to find her equilibrium in the moment.

"I am also well and sound, Miss Dragon," Samson chimed in merrily, enjoying the happy reunion his fortunate hail had created. "Pardon me, I meant Miss Kent, of course."

"It's Mr. Guilford, isn't it?" Olivia's greeting was cursory recalling him now from their fateful excursion to the *RavenSong*. "What brings you into town with Miss Aylesbury, Mr. Guilford?"

"Just putting together another care basket for Lady Claire's poor brother," he answered cheerfully.

Claire intervened, "Let's not have this conversation in the middle of the sidewalk, Olivia. Isn't there someplace more private nearby? A restaurant or tea house?"

"There is a tea house just across the lane. You're right, of course," Olivia sounded almost humble, "I should have been more discreet."

Blind Aphrodite

Samson escorted them both proudly, unaware of the strange agony in Claire's midsection at unexpectedly facing the chief conspirator against her happiness. The tea house owner was only too pleased to accommodate them with a private room that opened into a small courtyard. Money was scarce for luxuries, and his business had suffered with the revolution and the tariffs on English commodities.

As soon as he left the tray, Claire found herself unable to control her anger any longer. "I found Edward, Olivia." Her voice shook with rage. "How could you do this to me? How could you know that he was in danger, and try to convince me that he was dead?"

"Because I loved you both! Edward's letter begged me not to reveal his fate, commanded me not to risk the estates and what he thought was your only hope for a future."

"So all of you decided to just leave him to rot on a prison barge?" Claire demanded.

"No! I sent money and most of my wages to try to help him, but the couriers must have been dishonest. Imagine my horror when we arrived and realized that none of the money had reached him! I would have done anything to help him. I thought I *was* helping him by following his instructions and taking care of you!" Olivia moved to sit next to Claire, a rustle of silk petticoats and the scent of her perfume announcing her arrival.

"He *wrote* to you and you never told me!" Claire's grip on her cane was white-knuckled.

"Not directly—It doesn't matter, Claire!" Olivia's tears renewed their fall and she plunged ahead, "You may decide never to forgive me, but I only did what I thought best and what your own brother had sworn me to do. Oh, how worried we've been! Lord Forthglade has been beside himself with fear when you disappeared. We raced here, sure that you would arrive soon and hoping that we wouldn't be too late!"

"We?" the question was calm, and Claire knew the answer even before she asked it.

"Lord Forthglade and I, of course! I would have followed you alone, but Lord Forthglade insisted that he come too. He blames himself for pushing his suit and driving you away to such drastic measures. You must at least see him, Claire, and reassure him that you are all right!" Olivia covered her charge's gloved hands with her own. "He stays at the Lions Gate Inn."

Claire was stunned to silence at the twists and turns of fate.

Olivia took opportunity of Claire's lack of reply, "Where are you staying in the city?" She gasped, as if a terrible thought had just come to her, "Not on board that horrible ship with that—that pirate?"

"Hey!" Samson's protest reminded both women of his presence in the room. "I'll not have you speak ill of—"

Claire raised her hand to cut him off understanding the desire to defend his beloved ship and captain, "Olivia! Captain Grayson is most definitely not a pirate! If you must know I am staying at the Garden Street Inn, but I am not inviting you to call. I don't know if I can ever forgive you for your part in this. You could have pleaded ignorance about Edward's whereabouts without trying to convince me that he was dead!"

"I had heard a rumor of another plague on the *Laconia*! I assumed the worst and it was stupid of me." Olivia seemed to try to gather her strength, "Again, how can I tell you how much pain this has caused me?"

Claire felt some of her defenses fall at the sincere cry and wondered if anyone were really to blame. No one seemed to feel as if they had any choice in the matter.

"I knew you were desperate to find Edward," Olivia continued. "But how could you just run off with a complete stranger like that? Claire, your reputation! Oh, dearest! He hasn't compromised you, has he?"

Claire's cheeks flooded with heat at the bald question that she couldn't answer and it was then that Samson finally lost his temper. "The Captain's

Blind Aphrodite

a gentleman of the first cut whose blood is bluer than yours, you wicked harpy! How dare you even think such a thing! Just because a man don't wear silk drawers and heels don't make him a scoundrel! Take it back, witch, or I'll—"

Olivia's gasp of protest was ignored as Claire stood to take charge, "Mr. Guilford, please escort me back to the Inn. I need to drop off my purchases, and I have a headache from the day's events."

"Gladly, Lady Claire. Good day, Miss Dragon." Samson offered his arm crisply, and Claire clung to it for support as they turned to leave.

"Wait! Claire, wait," Olivia's plea stopped her with its quiet intensity.

Samson began to pull Claire along, but she turned in his grip to face the woman who was once a great friend. Something in Olivia's voice made Claire feel wary and frightened. *Be brave,* she heard Rutger's voice and held her ground. "Wait for me outside the door, Samson."

"But—" Samson was not about to leave her alone with a woman he now considered dangerous, but Claire accepted no arguments. She freed her hand from his arm, and stood away from him.

"Only a moment, Samson, please," Claire waited until she heard his sigh of compliance and the door close behind him. "Only a moment, Olivia."

"If I said I was sorry again, it would only be another useless apology for wrongs my soul can't even begin to fathom. But this one point I must have your forgiveness on or no other." It was the Olivia of old who seemed to be speaking to her now. Her voice was soft and open, without any edge or chilling bite. It was the voice of the woman who had held her when she had cried, and comforted her when she was ill. "Grayson helped you. He knew nothing of the situation, and you are grateful to him for bringing you to Edward's side. I don't know why I can't see past—past his appearance. I'm trying to see Grayson as you must see him, but I don't know if I can. Does that make me evil, Claire? I hate myself for the way he makes me feel. He is beyond gruesome, Claire. Half of his face would frighten a gargoyle." Olivia choked a little but went on, "He looks like he's sneering—a murderous demon."

"That's more than enough, Olivia." Claire didn't want to hear this. Her image of Rutger was many things, and she refused to have it tainted by Olivia's words.

"No, I'm afraid there's more." Olivia's voice broke and Claire's heart contracted at the sound. "Everyone else is flawed but you, Claire. Everyone else is blind, how is this possible? Don't you remember the beggar in the common gardens?"

"The—the common gardens?" Numbness began to creep into Claire's hands.

"In London, outside your Uncle Trevor's townhouse. It was the year of your debut, just weeks before the fever. Your first season was almost finished."

"Olivia, please stop." Claire could only whisper past a closed throat. This was a memory she had lost along the way, and now would give anything for mercy from Olivia and the past.

"Why, Claire? Because it would make you human to admit this?" Olivia's voice was still soft, but unrelenting. "You made us call the constable. He frightened you and they removed him. A poor old man with deformed limbs who probably had his nose cut off for picking pockets to survive."

"I was young and foolish," the defense rang hollow in her Claire's ears.

"Yes, and he was different than your valiant pirate, but still I wonder." Olivia came closer to gently take her trembling free hand. "Now do you condemn me for reacting to a man who has the face of Lucifer who practically kidnapped you? For worrying about a woman alone on a ship of hardened men crossing the Atlantic? For fearing for your virtue with a man who can only see you as a golden opportunity to gain a fortune and a woman's favors?"

Blind Aphrodite

Claire said nothing and at last, Olivia spoke again. "This then, at least, you forgive, Claire?"

"This, yes." And it was Olivia who sailed past her to signal Samson that Claire was finally ready to go.

* * *

"She's a harpy and a witch, I tell you!" Samson had a full head of steam now and Rutger knew better than to try to correct him. "I am swearing off spirited women after this bitter taste! She's an adder, and God only knows what poison she inflicted on our Claire when they were alone."

"*Our* Claire?" Rutger asked with a bitter smile. "I'm afraid even Claire would object to that title, my friend. A more independent creature has never walked."

"Bah!" Samson scoffed, "You're both stubborn and stupid. The witch said that some fancy named Forthglade was in port coming to offer his 'support' and my guess is more likely he hopes to bring her home a wife."

Rutger's jaw tightened at the news, wondering if Forthglade were the same 'odious man' Claire had said she was trying to escape in London. "She will turn to Edward for guidance and I'm sure her brother will do what's best for her."

"Her brother is an idiot! You said so yourself after seeing him on the *Laconia!*"

"Never mind what I said!" Rutger rose to his feet to face Samson's glare head-on, "We have no claim to this business! What am I waiting for, Samson? The British command to notice that it has a mercenary ship just idling at the docks? For another illegal blockade run to commit suicide? Shall I kidnap 'our Claire' from her troubles and take her into our next battle?"

Samson's eyes dropped, unable to face the pain in Muck's.

"Yes! What a splendid idea!" Rutger went on with an empty laugh, "I'll just keep her as a beloved pet until I find her on the gun deck and watch her get torn to pieces when a cannon misfires. I'll hold her in my arms and then wonder whose parts belong to whom, whose bones, whose blood?"

"Don't!" Samson reached for him, but Rutger struck his arm away.

"I love her, Samson." Golden eyes filled with tears. "So, tell me again who's the idiot?"

There were no words that could comfort, and Samson finally left him alone in a room that would never again be a sanctuary to Rutger's broken heart.

Chapter Eighteen

◯

The bath was luxurious, steaming hot water and scented oils soothing away the strain of an endless day. Claire closed her eyes and tried to shut out every thought but one. Edward was alive. It was the only good to come out of her entire 'adventure' and she put her face in her hands as the reality of her journey's end struck her. She was right back where she had started—blind, cornered into marriage, without a protector and any chance for independence lost. Worse, she had lost her heart along the way to Rutger and managed to bungle the affair beyond repair. He cared for her, but they had never spoken of the conditions that divided them. Now it was too late.

A knock at the door, and Bess entered to help her finish her toiletries. "There! You look all the better for lying down for a few minutes, and a bath was just the thing." Bess' gentle hands helped her from the water, and into her dressing gown. "Dinner is almost ready, and if you don't eat I'll be forced to tell cook! She's mighty temperamental, so unless you want eel paste the rest of your visit, you'd best mind me."

"I shall do my best, Bess." Claire answered with a mischievous grin. "Of course, I've never tasted eel paste before."

"I'm too fond of you to wish it, miss," Bess teased. "But I can have cook send a batch over to Sir Basil if you'd like." Their laughter was a welcome change for Claire, and she settled at the vanity table while Bess began to expertly brush out her long hair. Bess instinctively kept the conversation light, asking nothing of the day but chattering about the flowers that were blooming and how their honey supply was overflowing in the pantry. A soft knock at the door and Molly peeked a shy head through, "A gentleman downstairs to see you, m'lady, a Lord Philip Forthglade by name. I bid him wait in the private parlor."

"Good girl!" Bess praised. "The sun is setting, and we'll not have strange men knocking about our halls." She turned her attention to a somber Claire. "Will you see this rover, miss?"

Claire started to say no, but realized that sooner or later she would have to face him. "Tell him I will be down shortly." Molly giggled acknowledgement and closed the door.

"Well, we'd best get you presentable then." Bess moved to choose something suitable from her wardrobe, her hand resting on the sapphire-blue silk. "Your dark blue, miss?"

"Bess?" Claire's uncertain tone caught Bess' attention immediately.

"Yes, m'lady."

"Will you stay outside the door while I meet Lord Forthglade? Will you wait for me?" the question betrayed her fears, but Bess was quick to comfort.

"For as long as you need me, m'lady. Perhaps even longer if you like."

She entered the parlor minutes later hoping she appeared regal and brave in her dark blue silks. She left Bess at the door, and relied on her cane to cross the threshold safely. "Lord Forthglade?"

"Miss Aylesbury!" he sounded surprised to see her, and he crossed to formally take her hand and bow. "I am feeling more than a little foolish, I confess."

"Foolish?" it was not the start she had expected.

"If you knew the speeches I have practiced, and how angry I have been with everyone's scheming to push us together, and now I am staring at you like an idiot. And worse, admitting it!" his laugh was warm and clear.

Blind Aphrodite

"If I could see, I would have caught you staring, so perhaps you could count it as a gesture of honesty." She offered trying to be objective in light of her situation.

"Come and sit then, and I will try to at the very least, be honest with you."

"I would like that very much, Lord Forthglade." It was a vast understatement after weeks of deception, and Claire gratefully took the seat he offered and waited for what she assumed would be the pressing of his case for their marriage.

"I met your Uncle on business, and first met you at a Spring Ball. I thought you were charming, but Miss Kent forbid me to speak to you. She's formidable, isn't she?"

Claire nodded in agreement, "She can be."

His voice was warm and sincere, "I've caught glimpses of you since, and tried to make my honorable intentions known to your Uncle, but my timing has been cursed. Worse, I began to feel roped into a well-meaning ambush by your companion. No offense, but this has likely been the oddest courtship in recorded history." He laughed and Claire found herself smiling.

"But I insist on clearing things up right away, Miss Aylesbury." His voice dropped, as he grew serious. "I never wanted to surprise you like this. Miss Kent came to me in a complete panic and convinced me that you were in real trouble. She told me about the reason behind her maniacal matchmaking efforts, and I thought the least I could do was try to help your brother and hopefully shield you from Miss Kent."

"How brave of you," Claire found herself liking Philip, in spite of everything that had happened. In all the months that his name had been pressed on her, she had never really spoken to him before. The Spring Ball had been her first grand social event after losing her sight, and she remembered little of the evening except sheer terror and aching feet. At later awkward social gatherings, Olivia tended to guide her about like a dog on a short leash, and she had simply shut him out along with everyone else. "Miss Kent is certainly not to be underestimated."

"I never underestimate anyone, Miss Aylesbury." His voice was light again. "I must say that of all the people I know who might truly need a companion or 'guide', you don't strike me as one of them."

"Thank you, Lord Forthglade," Claire colored at this supreme compliment. "I have been trying to convince my family of that very thing. I have realized that well-meant guidance in particular, is something I may be better off without."

"You are her employer, you realize?"

"Pardon?" the simple question caught Claire off-guard.

"Miss Kent. You are her employer, yes?" he clarified his inquiry.

"Well, yes," she wondered what he intended, "Of course, my uncle actually hired—"

"Miss Aylesbury," he broke in, "Perhaps it isn't my place to say this but you can do anything you want to do. Let Miss Kent go. Ignore what people are telling you to do and trust your own instincts. Dismiss her, provide for your brother, and await him in England, whatever you want. You are a woman with a vast fortune, and you don't need to be babied. Although I can tell you that it is difficult not to want to protect you, especially from people like Miss Kent."

Claire was in shock, unsure of how to respond when he went on.

"I admire your spirit, Miss Claire, and would hate to see anyone or anything try to diminish or contain it." Philip sounded slightly gruff with embarrassment at his own speech.

"You are so kind," Claire exclaimed.

"Well, I can assure you that wasn't one of the speeches I imagined myself giving in this instance!" She heard him stand, and rose in response. "I should go, Miss Aylesbury. It is inappropriate to be here at the dinner hour."

Blind Aphrodite

"Would you accept an invitation to stay for the evening meal then?" she offered.

"You are too kind, but I'm afraid I have another engagement with a cousin." He sounded as if he regretted going, "But I wanted to take this opportunity to tell you that I have been little involved in these schemes and am sorry for the impression you must have to the contrary. If you need help arranging a transport home, or if there is something I can do for you or for your brother here, please let me know."

"Thank you, Lord Forthglade," Claire offered her hand and he took it cordially only to hold it a few seconds beyond convention.

"One last thing, since I am attempting only honesty," he took a deep breath, "My proposal of marriage still stands. I just didn't want you to doubt my true feelings."

He left her in bemused astonishment and Bess came in quickly to check on her favorite guest. "Was he fresh, miss?"

Claire smiled at the tone that reminded her of Samson. "He was a perfect gentleman." The demon had proven to be sincerely charming and all that was kind. Perhaps she had discovered an ally after all.

Chapter Nineteen

☯

Philip Trent leaned back in the cushioned seat of his carriage and gloried in the laughter that rolled from his belly. It had been a virtuoso performance! No thanks to his idiot cousin and the whore's misinformation, he had almost missed a deadly turn in the road. But his clever tigress had saved the day. A visit to the jailer, a small bribe paid and Philip had learned the gist of the tender scene between twin brother and sister. Philip was ecstatic, as the conversation couldn't have been scripted more advantageously to his schemes. Of course, he hadn't shared this tidbit with Olivia, preferring to use her like the game warden that drives the prey towards the hunter. As Olivia pushed and unknowingly played the villain, he gained a vast advantage with Claire by pretending to side with her against 'them'.

His laughter quieted as he recalled the one potential snag in his smooth path to marital bliss. Grayson was still in port, and was not to be trusted not to interfere. He had played 'hero' once to help Claire find her long lost brother. He could yet offer her a shoulder to cry on and potentially another avenue of escape. Philip's plan was only guaranteed of success if his were the only sympathetic voice she could hear. And so it was time at last to introduce himself to the notorious captain of the *RavenSong* and to give the man the push he needed to set sail.

    ✶   ✶   ✶

Blind Aphrodite

Rutger stretched his legs out to rest his heels against the now cold stove. He lazily rolled a full glass of whiskey in his hands, warming its amber contents while he stared up at the ceiling of his quarters. It was apparently the only space in the room that didn't hold a tormenting memory of Claire. A glance to the left afforded him a view of the door to a room he still considered 'hers'. An unfortunate glance to the right only brought the carved posts of his bed into view. Other directions offered the library he had offered to share with her, the table where they took their meals, the window seats where she had sunned herself like a cat, the list was endless. Staring at the ceiling was a temporary solution at best he realized, but any thread of peace he could grab was worth the effort.

Samson's knock broke into his reverie, and he stood to go open the door. "Samson, I'm in no mood for company."

"Then you'll not be pleased to hear this, Muck." Samson wasted no time with apologies, "There's a Philip Trent, the seventh Lord Forthglade at the plank asking to see you."

"You're not serious," Rutger's growl made Samson take a friendly step back.

"I'll tell him you're not taking callers at the moment," Samson made an abrupt turn happy to send the fancy gentleman packing.

"By all means, bring him in, Samson." Rutger's words halted Samson's progress.

"I won't! It was stupid of me to tell you he was here in the first place. You've nothing to gain from this conference, and I don't like the way he looks."

"Get-him-or-I'll-go-get-him-myself." Each word came through gritted teeth and Samson gave in with a huge sigh.

"You'll kindly remember later that I advised against this," and he headed off to do his captain's bidding.

Renee Bernard

Rutger walked back into his quarters, leaving the door wide open for his 'guest'. He looked out the open window onto the moonlit harbor, his back to the room's entrance. One shot of whiskey for false courage and Rutger relished the burning warmth of it in his stomach. If nothing else, this would be an interesting test to see if he could still feel pain.

"Captain Grayson, I presume?" a voice like liquid silk and Rutger decided he hated him before he'd even turned around.

"At your service, Lord Forthglade." He faced his unexpected visitor and noted the lack of the usual reactions. Philip instead bowed politely and made his way into the room.

"Forgive me, Captain. It has been the longest of days, but I couldn't wait another hour to meet you and offer my sincere gratitude."

"Gratitude? For what exactly?" Rutger made an effort to keep his voice even, trying to gauge his opponent. Philip appeared to be every inch the titled English rake, the cut of his clothes were the height of fashion. He was in his early thirties, with dark coloring and flawless falcon-like features. He looked like the perfect foil to Claire's beauty and status, and Rutger's stomach clenched at the thought of it. Philip's expression was one of a man determined to complete his mission no matter what it takes.

"For looking after Miss Aylesbury," Philip's gaze was level to Rutger. "I wished to thank you for delivering her safely to Savannah."

"You're welcome," Rutger tossed back the rest of his glass before setting it down on the table. "Pleasure meeting you, Trent."

It was meant as a dismissal, but Philip shifted awkwardly and held his ground. "I wish the matter was concluded, but I'm afraid I have yet another favor to ask."

"A favor? I must say you are bold, sir." Rutger fought a genuine curiosity to discover Philip's intent. A grim inner voice reminded him that every favor he had ever been asked had led to his own ruin.

Blind Aphrodite

"I shall take that as a compliment, Captain." Philip replied with a warm smile that fell away as he came to the issue at hand. "I hope you won't misinterpret what I am about to say. It's just that you have been seen a great deal about town escorting Miss Aylesbury, even calling on her at her rooms at the Garden Street Inn. In light of the lack of a chaperon while on board this vessel, your continuing presence only further damages her reputation. For Claire's sake, I would ask you to avoid scandal and leave port immediately."

"For Claire's sake?" Rutger asked quietly.

"Make no mistake here, Captain." Philip was very still as he spoke, "I don't blame you for aiding her as you did. Claire is reckless and loves her brother very much. If I had known of his situation earlier, I would have taken her immediately to be at his side. An ill-timed lover's quarrel, Miss Kent's interference—the details don't concern you, Captain. In any case, Edward has now given his blessing for our match, and he has already spoken to Claire."

"Did he?" Rutger's bravado hid the sinking feeling of a man who has just gambled away his life's fortunes. The echo 'lover's quarrel' ricocheted in his chest, and Rutger considered having another drink.

"Yes, he did." Philip took a deep breath, "It was a formality really. I had already approached her Uncle in London and secured his approval."

"You apparently omitted to tell Claire. I'm afraid my impression of your relationship was vastly different."

Philip's expression was defiant, "And I'm afraid that your impression is of no concern to me. My only concern is the effect that your presence has on my fiancée's tenuous position."

"She—she has agreed to marry you?" Rutger's legs turned to lead at the question.

"I am pleased to say, yes." Philip seemed to relax at his happy announcement. "Congratulations are in order, but I won't hold it against you if you decline to send your felicitations."

Rutger was struck speechless, unprepared for the next cruel blow.

"I understand how you feel about Miss Aylesbury, sir." The sympathy in Philip's voice was acid in Rutger's ears. "I cast no blame. I heard you were quite a rake in your day. And I can see how Claire's sightlessness would hold an appeal to your wounded vanity."

"You understand nothing about my feelings, Forthglade." Rutger's growled fiercely.

Philip was not intimidated, "Really? Are you telling me that this venture was entirely for a noble cause? Are you telling me that she holds no appeal for you? That you don't find her uniquely charming? What man wouldn't wish to have such a beauty by his side?"

Rutger felt his control slipping and decided he had definitely failed the test as he discovered new levels of pain he hadn't realized existed. "She isn't 'sightless', Forthglade. She has a clear vision and a remarkable talent for reading a man's soul. You go too far in presuming what went on between us."

"Miss Aylesbury assured me that you were a perfect gentleman, and I have decided to accept her word." The look of determination returned to Philip's narrow features, "However, polite society is not as easily forgiving and so I have come to ask you to leave immediately so that we can begin our lives together without your shadow lurking behind her."

"Lurking?" the question sounded as hollow as Rutger's heart.

"Miss Aylesbury always had a soft heart for the less-fortunate, Captain. I certainly hope you won't continue to play on her weaknesses."

It was the last straw. "Get out, Forthglade."

"As you wish, Captain," he gave another courtly bow. "Bon voyage."

Chapter Twenty

As her hand found the rope guide for the *RavenSong's* gangplank, Claire marveled at how her life had made a vast circle in the last weeks. She stood for a moment only two steps up the walk to allow the rhythm of the tides help her recover her 'sea legs'. She remembered how terrifying this threshold had seemed only recently when she came to Rutger to ask him to save her life. She had trusted him completely, her instincts leading her back to him in her quest for the truth about Edward. Now, she sought him out again.

After hours of pacing in her room after Philip's departure wrestling with the future that hinged on her choices, a solution had come to her with stunning simplicity. Edward was ordering her to marry for protection. Philip had urged her to follow her instincts. The revelation had been like a stroke of lightening. And once she had the idea, everything seemed to fall into place. Rutger—she would marry Rutger and satisfy the demands of duty and her heart in one brilliant move. She was in love with him, and knew that he cared for her. Or at least, hoped that his feelings hadn't faded since that terrible night. The kiss in the carriage had given her hope. Whatever Olivia's impressions, she knew he had family of note. And it was irrelevant, considering her fortune. She smiled at the beauty of it. She was going to ask him to marry her.

A night breeze pulled at her full skirts, a sensuous whisper of silk against her legs. It was well after midnight, and she had managed to slip out unnoticed to hire a carriage. The sapphire-blue gown was one of her most flattering, according to Bess, but more importantly had front lacing over the stomacher to allow her to dress without alerting the maids to her plans. She only hoped that Rutger found it pleasing, and wasn't too shocked at her forward proposal. She had considered every argument against it, but was sure that he could be convinced.

At last, she felt comfortable with the swaying of the boards beneath her feet and using the rope and her cane as a guide, made it up the short walk. The ship was quiet, and she tiptoed carefully across the deck to avoid waking what sounded like a sleeping Mr. Sweet on watch in the forecastle. She had little need for the cane, familiar with the ship and its layout from countless walks on her decks. The companionway wasn't latched, and she reached the door to Rutger's quarters quickly. It was only then that her courage faltered. But Claire raised her chin in determination, giving a silent admonition to all the doubts and fears that clamored for a hasty retreat. She knocked softly on the door and then waited.

The door opened immediately and startled her. "Captain? I was afraid I would have woken you at this late hour." There was a strange pause, and Claire started to take a step back, "Captain?"

"Come in, Claire," he grabbed her wrist and pulled her gently into the room. "What brings you to the ogre's garden so late at night?"

His voice was thicker than usual, but her attention was caught by his words. "Ogre? Rutger, please don't say that—"

He released her hand and stood close. "Muck." The word held a universe of pain.

"What did you say, Rutger?" she ached at the sound of it on his lips reaching up to hold his face in her hands as she had in the carriage. At the touch, she realized she had left her gloves behind and bare fingers traced the heat of his skin and cupped his chiseled jaw. The odd lines and contours of his left cheek held the same warmth as the smooth plane of his right cheek, and Claire marveled at the beauty of him.

Blind Aphrodite

"Muck." He spoke softly. "It's a name, Claire. It's my name, actually. No one calls me Rutger anymore." He closed the space between them as his hands gently framed her face. "Before the accident, Rutger. After the accident, Muck. You see the difference?"

The scent of whiskey crept into her awareness, but she tried to focus on what Rutger was saying. "Rutger, I don't—"

"Say it, Claire. Just once before you go, I want to hear you say my name." His voice was sorrow.

"I'm not going anywhere." She tipped her face back, aching now with his pain but also with her own longing. Her hands fell to his shoulders and brazenly traced the smooth planes of his chest to the curve of his arms.

"Please." The weight of his plea was unfathomable to her and she knew she could never refuse him.

"Muck," she said it quietly, hating the sound but sensing the change in him. The tender embrace became charged with desire, and Claire felt a new tension in him as he slowly pulled her against him.

"Tell me no, Claire." A hoarse plea that made her heart pound. "Just tell me no."

She knew she should stop this, make him understand that she had found a way for them to be together always. But then his lips found hers and she knew nothing but the sensation of his touch. Her desire for him had never diminished and after endless days and nights of denial, her body now demanded fulfillment. His kiss was gentle and tasted of oak and spirits, and it was Claire who took more, arching against him until she was breathless from the fire of his mouth on hers.

Whatever rein he had held on his passion was gone as Claire urged him to take all that she offered. He released her from his kiss, only to lift her and carry her towards the bed. She felt a strange flutter of anxiety as her feet left the floor, and she dropped her cane. It was so wonderful to be held, almost weightless in his embrace, but she blushed to recall her last moments under the canopy of his great bed. A grave whisper in her ear broke into her muddled thoughts, "Only if you wish it, Claire." He set her down gently on the bed, standing above her but leaving her free of his touch.

She felt lost without his hands and the heat of him against her. "I wish only for you. Marry me." She reached out to pull him closer expecting him to crush her against him, but her beloved captain had other plans.

"So beautiful, " he murmured against her throat, gently easing her back against the soft mattress. "You're so incredibly beautiful." His kisses were slow and deep, pulling her into a sweet storm of his making. His tongue traced the contours of her swollen lips, tasting her need. He kissed a hot path to her ears and then down her throat, a lazy journey that made her gasp as her blood quickened. His mouth teased past the sensitive hollow of her neck and shoulders, down the creamy expanse of her breasts to the prim neckline of her dress.

He growled playfully against her skin and then his hand slid up from where it had been resting against her waist. She groaned as his palm swept over the ample swell of her breasts—soft chafing of his hands through the silk making them taut beneath his fingers. The front-laces that had allowed her to dress unaided now provided him with all the assistance he needed as he began pulling loose her ties. He tasted her mouth again as he finished the laces, and freed her from the confines of the bodice and stomacher. He rose to kneel on the bed and lifted her to face him, the gown slipping from her shoulders. With strong hands, he swept the material down her curves deliberately pulling the silk texture in luxurious friction against her sensitive skin, the cool night air making her shiver.

She instinctively moved to shield herself from his gaze, but he lightly swept her hands away and drew her back into his arms. The gown fell to her waist, and Rutger pulled her against his chest and then back down onto the bed. Claire felt wanton and daring as his hands began skillfully peeling away her petticoats one by one. With each layer he removed, his

Blind Aphrodite

hands explored her exposed skin and his mouth sampled her trembling curves. Finally she lay beside him divested of all her garments, vulnerable and artless in her desire. "Please—" she quietly asked an unfinished question she didn't entirely understand, but knew that the answer would be found in his arms.

"A magic word, Claire," his voice was as arousing as his touch, "Even ogres know it."

Claire drew breath to protest Rutger calling himself an ogre, but found herself gasping at the contact of his hand now guiding hers. He pulled her hands toward the loose ties of his own shirt and slid her hand across the feverish skin of his chest. The invitation was clear, and Claire followed his touch eagerly, untying his shirt and exploring the shape of him. He lay still, allowing her to grow accustomed to this freedom and Claire reveled in the sense of control and power that flooded through her. Desire to know him fully surpassed her modesty as male beauty was revealed through her fingertips. She pulled the shirt from him, hungry for the touch of his bare skin against hers. Imitating his own touch, she began to trace kisses down his chest, daring to dart her tongue lightly over his hard nipples. She was rewarded by the groan of pleasure that escaped him, and became even bolder as her hands delicately mapped the muscular landscape of his stomach. Her courage faltered as her fingers reached his belt, but passion allowed no retreat.

Strong hands guided hers to the rigid length of his need and she gasped at the raw power that throbbed beneath her touch. Tea-room gossip and whispers, veiled comments from married ladies had given her only a vague notion of male anatomy, but the reality of his arousal intensified her awareness of just how far she had come. And how much farther she now longed to venture.

She lost track of whose fingers were hers, but the belt buckle fell away under their hands, his leather leggings shed and then there was nothing between them as his body covered hers. He held himself above her, once again making her breathless with his mouth against hers until he began again to blaze a tantalizing trail of delicious kisses down her body. Now there was no dress to halt his progress, and Claire moaned as he found each sensitive place with his tongue, savoring her reactions before moving lower.

When she was sure that he would relent, she gasped in shock as his mouth found the hot junction between her legs, his tongue teasing her into a molten flame. She writhed at the intensity of sensations that began to race through her frame, unsure if she could withstand their release. His stroke quickened, and she cried out as the climax overtook her, each sweet wave making her shiver against his hands.

"Rutger?" She had barely formed the word, and his arms were around her with his body pressed against hers. At the brush of his rigid member against her thighs, she instinctively understood that there was more to be experienced in their union. His soft words and the return of his mouth to hers conquered a small flutter of fear. She gave herself over to the renewed ardor of his touch and the passion it aroused. He parted her legs gently with his own and pressed into the heat that beckoned him onward. The rhythm of movement increased, and Claire countered it naturally, pushing him over the edge of his tight control.

She felt her body yield to his until a barrier was reached, and then suddenly the tempo and force of his movements changed, and Claire cried out as he drove into her completely, unprepared for the sharp pain. Even as she tensed against him, he held motionless and soothed her with kisses. "Shhhh," a ragged whisper in her ear seemed to share her pain, "Never hurt you, Claire. Never again."

Even as he spoke, the pain seemed to fall away as a new awareness of the tight burning pleasure of his hardened member now sheathed within her took its place. Slowly, he began to move again and this time she found herself sighing at the sweet friction of it, at the sultry irony of both having and wanting. She caught the rhythm rapidly, unable to get enough of

Blind Aphrodite

his touch and the taste of him in her mouth. Tenderness melted into passion, and Claire felt the first relentless pull of her own release as each stroke moved deeper until he was a part of her soul.

His breathing quickened, mirroring her own until she cried out with ecstasy, unaware of the climax that seized them both as Rutger's release surged to meet hers. Claire wasn't sure how many seconds or minutes passed as she clung to him while lingering pulses of energy ebbed away. The world disappeared beyond the protective canopy of her captain's ornate bed, and Claire's heart relished the weight of him against her and the emotions he invoked. Claire marveled at how serene she felt, how complete. "I love you." The words were bravely whispered before she realized it.

"Only in a monster's dreams," he growled against her hair, the words slurred. "Now hush." As he held her closely their legs entwined and Claire relinquished the battle against the contentment and peace that coursed through her. After endless sleepless nights and anxiety filled days, everything faded against the sound of his heartbeat and Claire fell fast asleep.

* * *

"Where were you?" Olivia demanded before Philip had even begun to remove his coat.

At first he seemed determined to ignore her, humming a simple tune and positively brimming with contentment. At last, he turned to give her his complete attention, "How many times do I have to tell you not to ask me too many questions, tigress?"

"Did you see her tonight? Has Edward urged her to accept you? Have you asked her to elope?" She gave him a sarcastic smile, "Too many questions, my lord?"

The sound of his hand striking her face was like a rifle shot in the small room. His own expression of contentment never wavered.

Renee Bernard

"Ph-Philip, don't!" Olivia stumbled back, a pale hand reaching up as if to verify the existence of the stinging print of his fingers across her cheek.

"Why not?" He crossed the room to take a seat on the small settee, and began to take off his leather boots. "I thought you liked it?"

Olivia felt a roar of pain from behind the wall inside of her and she stiffened her spine against the dark weakness that threatened to overwhelm her. "What I would like, Philip, is for this business to be over. I want to be with you! To be Lady Forthglade as you promised! Let's finish this, Philip! There isn't much time—"

"Don't be stupid! Claire trusts me, and Grayson is probably making plans to drop his lines and make for the open ocean at first light. Especially after my inspiring visit to him this evening." With his boots removed, he leaned back to present the perfect picture of relaxation. "When he strands her here, she is mine. I have all the time in the world."

"Philip, there is something you should know." She whispered, hoping against reason that Philip would help her hold back the void.

"No, tigress." His eyes looked like flat obsidian in the room's light. "There isn't."

"I'm carrying your child, Philip."

Time spun out as Olivia stood before him; her eyes shining with unshed tears and her white skin revealing the first shadows of a bruise across her face. "Mine? Really? I wouldn't be so sure."

"How can you say that to me? After everything we've meant to each other. After everything I've done…allowed you to do to me—"Her throat closed as ghostly images seem to gather just beyond her vision. Hands that had held her down, and Philip smiling just as he was at this moment—watching.

"Your assumptions make you easy to control, Olivia. I never said I would marry you. You did make a delicious mistress, but how could I possibly make a slut like you the next Lady Forthglade?"

"No!" It was a protest without any force behind it as she clawed against invisible tides to keep the memories at bay.

"This bastard of yours is the last straw, Olivia. Tiresome of you, really. Let me make one thing perfectly clear. You'll stay out of my way while I conclude my courtship, or I'll denounce you for the murderess you are."

"Murderess?" Her vision cleared to take in his ruthless and handsome features.

"Basil just received word from a ship's dispatch this morning. The Duke of Danbury is dead." Philip managed to look slightly moved at this ominous news, but the twinkle in his eyes betrayed his mirth.

"But I didn't! The powder was just to keep him weak you said! You said it was just to keep him—" Olivia felt as if she were trapped in a nightmare. She was the mother of his child! The woman who had given him everything to achieve their dreams! The betrayal had come too soon, and Olivia's schemes to bind him to her disintegrated.

"It was slow poison, and the vials are still in your rooms in London. Cross me and I'll send anonymous word to the authorities that will no doubt lead them to hang you. Now get out. I need to rest and change for my date with Miss Aylesbury."

"Philip?" One last plea for a hundred things she now realized that he would never give her.

"Did you want one last tumble, tigress?" He lunged at her suddenly from the cushions, uncoiling like a snake with all its deadly venom and intent. Olivia made no sounds as he began to brutally take her on the floor. She lay unmoving beneath him as the wall crumbled down at last and she blindly surveyed the ruins of her dreams.

Chapter Twenty-one

Claire's dreams dissipated gently and with the sway of the tides, she remembered where she was. She lay for a moment or two listening to Rutger's deep breathing as sleep held him captive. 'Compromised,' she recalled but discovered that no guilt accompanied the slight ache between her legs and the flood of provocative memories that made her cheeks color. The bright white blur that streaked her dark field of vision told her that it was full morning. She eased herself from the bed to find her clothes and dress quickly, fearing that one of the crew would look in on Rutger and discover her in her current state. Guilty or no, she felt intense modesty at the thought of being found nude by one of her shipmates.

She moved to her former room to dress and clean herself in the washstand. As she tied the laces on the bodice, she walked back into his quarters and stopped in her tracks. Re-entering the room, Claire became more and more aware of the smell of whiskey that permeated the air. He had been drinking last night, she knew, but now she began to wonder if she had underestimated how intoxicated he had been. Her chin raised as she dismissed new fears. 'I was certainly sober to know what I was doing,' she chided herself silently. 'It changes nothing.' But as she knelt to search for her bamboo stick, her hand knocked over the whiskey bottle that rested on the floor by his chair. She stopped it from rolling almost immediately, anxious not to awake Rutger. The cold, empty bottle in her fingers grew heavier and heavier as her thoughts began to turn over it's meaning.

Blind Aphrodite

She had come to discuss a proposal of marriage, but she realized that there had in fact been very little 'discussion' in the course of events. She had thrown herself wantonly into his arms, ignoring his offer of restraint. She had told him that she loved him, she had asked him to marry her. He had never said 'yes'. But his actions seemed to convey agreement, didn't they? Her hand located her discarded cane and she stood to straighten her skirts. She considered waking him, but his even breathing convinced her that he may still be suffering from the effects of the bottle and that it was likely no use.

'It's simple,' she lectured her trembling limbs. 'I'll just wait till he's awake and then I will just restate my proposal. Rutger accepts, and then we'll—'There was a quick knock at the door and before Claire could react, Samson walked in and they both gave a startled cry. "I'm so sorry, Samson," she began with a shaky laugh. "I'm afraid I wasn't watching where I was walking."

"Lady Claire! What the devil are you doing here?" his tone was one of total shock and Claire straightened with embarrassment at how things must appear to her friend.

"Shhh! He's sleeping!" She indicated Rutger, her cheeks aflame.

"Would you mind stepping into the companionway then?"

Claire stepped out, taking deep breaths to tame her nerves. "I—I came to see Rutger to—"

"We're friends, aren't we?" Samson began without prelude.

"Of course, Samson." Claire answered without hesitation.

"And we both care for Muck."

"I wish you wouldn't call him that, Sam—"

"Do you mean to kill him? To destroy any last chance the man has for peace of mind? How many times can a man survive having his heart wrecked?

"Samson!" Claire was astonished. "I have no intentions of wrecking his heart. I came to tell him that—"

"Bah! Intentions!" Samson was unimpressed.

"—I'm staying with him, Mr. Guilford." She finished breathlessly, sure that this misunderstanding would now be clear.

"It's impossible!" Samson sounded mournful but resolute. "Your family would never consent. And this isn't a floating pleasure barge, Lady Claire. This is a mercenary ship and if you think we're going to take you into our next scuffle or be sent to the scaffold for your kidnapping, you are sadly mistaken."

"Rutger isn't a mercenary! I can't believe you're saying this." It was as if she were speaking to a complete stranger. "He is a trader and a merchant."

"Believe what you will, mistress," Samson was relentless. "I was wrong to have encouraged this foolishness in the first place. We've played the role of valiant heroes, and for what? An empty cargo hold, dangerous shore leave surrounded by soldiers, and the compensation of watching Muck consumed by self-hate? I care for you, too, but as far as Muck's concerned you're more destructive than any cannon."

"How can you say that? Surely you know that I would never—"Claire faltered, unsure of what she was promising as her thoughts raced to keep up with the pounding of her heart. Mercenaries—how could it be true? Samson was dug in like a badger protecting his beloved captain, and all her own doubts seem to support his cause.

"I only know that the last of the crew will be returning from shore leave soon enough, and then it won't matter. The captain has already given orders to prepare to leave. Wait here, and I'll have Mallory fetch you a carriage back to the Inn. Miss Dragon came by this morning probably looking for you, so you'd best come up with a convincing tale as to your whereabouts." He took a deep breath. "If you love him, Lady Claire, you'll let the man recover what is left of his life—and his heart."

Blind Aphrodite

Sure that she would obey his commands, he left her in the companionway to find Mallory.

Claire was stunned as she leaned against the paneled wall for support. Samson was asking her to leave the ship. In defending the captain, his words had impacted like bombs. She wasn't sure what to think as she stood only two steps from Rutger's door. Was he the hero or the villain in a fairy-tale of her own making? She had proposed marriage to a pirate and possibly mistaken drunken lust for a lifetime's commitment. She had fallen in love with him, but had conjured his personal demons. He had saved her life, only to steal her heart. A night of passion, but Claire wondered how much of it had been her own delusions and blind-selfishness. She wanted him to rescue her, but at what cost to his own existence?

She crept back into his cabin and with the cadence of his breathing in the background left compensation for the pain she had inflicted for him to find after she'd gone. Tears streaming down her face, she returned to her place in the hallway like a chastened child to wait for Mallory and the humiliating ride back to her rooms.

✶   ✶   ✶

Rutger opened his eyes slowly with a groan. The whiskey had definitely been a mistake, he thought wryly. He had always taken pride in his self-control, but last night he had discovered that pride was no match for self-pity. His brow furrowed as he recalled strange fragments of a dream, something about ogres in a garden. Claire, he thought suddenly and winced at the erotic flavor of his fantasies. In the dream, she had come to him—Aphrodite in all her glory and without shame. Fleeting images gained momentum as Rutger's head started to clear. Dark blue silk, the creamy perfection of her skin, Claire's cry as he drove into her, the sound of his name on her lips. Rutger sat up with a jolt causing the room to spin around him for a few seconds.

The haze of alcohol lifted and the floodgates of suffering opened as he realized that the dream had been real. The precise details eluded him, but somehow Claire had come to the *RavenSong* last night to see him and instead had been attacked by a drunken monster. A glance at the sheets that pooled at his waist confirmed his worst nightmare. Bloodstains glared back at him, and Rutger felt as if he were watching the scene from some great distance. She had probably come to personally tell him about her engagement to Philip—she had said something about marriage, hadn't she? And then...he wasn't entirely sure what had happened next, but the end result was indisputable. He had bedded her, thoroughly by the look of it. He put his pounding head into his hands for a minute, trying to make sense of the incomprehensible. His recollection didn't feel like force was used, he couldn't believe that he was capable of such a thing. Although seducing an innocent and trusting woman wasn't something he would have believed either. Still, he was sure that that was exactly what he must have done.

His hands dropped away from his face and he looked hopelessly around his empty quarters. He may have overwhelmed her defenses last night, but it was apparent that she had fled at first light, no doubt ashamed and disgusted by his behavior. All his promises to her, all his pledges of trust and care abandoned and decimated in one night.

He forced himself to get up and get dressed, his movement jerky with anger and self-revulsion. He wondered if Lord Forthglade would be calling with muskets to demand a gentleman's defense of his fiancée's honor. It would certainly be within the man's rights, but Rutger wasn't going to wait for Philip to provide restoration. Without realizing it, Rutger had chosen his old black boots and leggings and dark tailored coat and as he caught his reflection in the dressing mirror, he recognized Neptune's hermit. Clothed for shadows and frightening moonlit encounters, Rutger acknowledged that he looked like a handsome monster after all. A humorless smile completed

Blind Aphrodite

the image, and Rutger decided that he was ready to try to outrun the voices in his head.

A knock on the door made him draw the brocade curtains around the bed guiltily before hailing his visitor. "Come in, then."

Cutter entered cautiously, his eyes taking in his friend's attire and grim expression. "I brought you a tonic for your headache and the inventory lists you requested."

"Thank you, Cutter. You can just put the lists on my desk." Rutger came over to take the offered mug, and then froze. "How much does the ship know?"

"There's trouble in port and we'll need to be going." Cutter was having trouble meeting Rutger's intense gaze. "A murder at one of the dock's taverns. Samson has sent word to recall the men, just in case and to make sure we're well clear of the mess."

Rutger was distracted for only an instant. "None of my men were involved."

"Of course not! But if authorities are sweeping the area looking for suspicious characters, it's wise for us to stay close to the ship."

Silence met this explanation, and Cutter realized that the distraction had passed. "How much does the ship know?"

"It doesn't matter, Muck." Cutter shifted his weight uncomfortably.

"It matters to me," his golden eyes blazed and Cutter started to pray for a painless retreat.

"We know, Captain," Cutter decided honesty was the best course. "She must have come aboard in the night. Sweet is very upset and blames himself."

"Oh god," Rutger's mouth filled with the coppery taste of shame. "Did—did you see her leave?"

Cutter swallowed hard before answering, "Yes."

"And?"

"What is it that you want me to tell you, Captain?" Cutter sounded desperate. "That she was in tears? That I didn't see any bruises? That she looked fine? That you were drunk? That it wasn't your fault?"

"That's more than enough, Mr. Cutter." Rutger reeled away from him, groaning at the too quick movement that made his stomach roll.

"I agree, Muck. Enough blame, don't you think? You are in love with her, and there isn't a man on this earth that can't be pushed too far. Now stop this insane punishment and make a decision."

Rutger looked back in astonishment at his friend. "What?"

"I didn't know you before the accident. You brought me on board as ship's physician just after it. A precaution, I thought at the time, against future tragedies. I don't measure you against your past. I have the luxury of seeing you as you are." Cutter's voice was steady and strong. "The smuggling and the piracy are just ways of punishing yourself for sins you didn't really commit in the first place. Ironic, isn't it? And now she's brought you back to the threshold of civilization, and you're convinced that you aren't worthy to accept the invitation. A paradox."

"You should leave, Cutter." Rutger's eyes became cold and shuttered and he began to move towards his desk intending to busy himself with the paperwork that awaited him.

"Make a decision, Captain." Cutter left him to his lists.

Rutger moved unfeeling fingers across meaningless text until his hand came across a large lump under the parchment. He moved the pile aside and spotted an unfamiliar black velvet pouch with a silk cord drawstring. He lifted it carefully and its contents spilled out onto the table. Sunlight caught the diamonds in full glorious force and a rainbow of priceless color played before his eyes. Payment rendered, an empty cry seemed to echo through him. *Make a decision.* Rutger stood abruptly, his eyes locked on the glittering wealth that lay on the table. *Make a decision.* He nodded, sensing the first sharp drop in his chosen path. It was to be restoration after all.

Chapter Twenty-two

It was a subdued Claire that readied herself to visit Edward as Bess clucked over the fine material of the summer dress and her mistress' beautiful hair. If she had worried that Bess would see a difference in her, it passed quickly. Claire concentrated only on how black her dark world seemed today and how odd it was to say that 'love is blind.' Did the saying intend it as a blessing or a curse? Claire puzzled miserably that either meaning held no comfort for her.

At last, Bess finished her efforts to make her presentable and Claire began to gather her basket filled with much needed items for Edward. "Did you find the mittens, Bess?"

"Oh! I believe they're still in the trunk, miss." Bess' hurried steps told Claire she was eager to help. "Here they are," Bess brought them to Claire but then gave a little startled sound and Claire heard something metal fall to the floorboards and roll to her feet.

"What was that?" Claire stood still, not wanting to step on the lost item.

"A ring!" Bess' excitement at the unexpected discovery was contagious. She stooped to pick it up and handed it to Claire for examination. "A man's ring by the look of it! It must have been inside one of the mittens for safekeeping."

The weight of it in Claire's hand was familiar and her touch confirmed its meaning. "It's Edward's signet ring, with the crest of the family. He never took it off except…"

"Except?" Bess filled with curiosity urged her on.

"Send for a carriage, Bess." Claire dropped the ring into the deep pocket hidden in the folds of her skirt and picked up the basket. "I will leave immediately to see my brother."

She remembered little of the carriage ride to the port jail, grateful only for a few moments alone to consider what the day might bring. As the carriage halted, the driver stepped down to help her to the door before she paid him in coin. Claire took one last deep breath of fresh air before entering the stale interior of the prison.

The jailer recognized her easily from the previous day and even seemed pleased to see her. "He's been waiting for you, miss. Another basket?"

"Just a few more items for John, sir. Would you care to inspect them?" She held out the basket handle sure he would now help himself to its contents.

"You haven't the look of a dangerous woman, miss. I'll have your word there's no weapon amidst your baked goods and woolens?" He growled as a matter of form, but she heard no threat in his words.

"You have my word, sir." And at that, he offered her his arm and began to lead Claire down the hallway to the prisoner's cells and Edward. The sound of the keys and tumbler heralded her entrance, and Edward's voice was like a balm to her weary nerves.

"Claire!" They embraced and she tried to reassure herself that no matter what happened she would not lose her brother. "One night and I began to wonder if I'd imagined your visit."

Memories of how she had spent the night made the heat rise to her cheeks and she hoped that Edward was not able to read her expression. "Don't be foolish, John." She slid her cane into her free hand and found the small table. "I've brought yet another treasure trove. They will let you keep everything, won't they?"

"Yes, I believe so." His voice didn't convey the confidence he intended, but there was nothing else to say. "Claire, come and sit with me. There isn't much time."

Blind Aphrodite

"We have several minutes left, and I will come again tomorrow!" she soothed, sitting at the table with him while he held her hands in his own.

"No, Claire," Edward's voice was unsteady with emotion. "I am to be returned to the ship tonight. Although, the jailer said my quarters there will improve now that I have a patron."

"Tonight? It's too soon!" It was a cruel surprise after everything that had happened. "Patron?"

"They haven't identified him to me, but I have no doubt as to who has been making arrangements on my behalf. Claire, have you given thought to Lord Forthglade's proposal?" His grip on her fingers tightened with the urgency of his question.

"I have thought of little else since yesterday." Claire hesitated, "But you must know that it was Captain Grayson who arranged for you to leave the prison ship, not Lord Forthglade. If you press Philip's suit because you believe he—"

"Claire, it was Lord Forthglade who made the arrangements. I have his word on this. As for Grayson, I'm not going to waste these moments arguing about his lack of motive or worth." She heard the stubborn tone and found it all too familiar.

"You're wrong about Rutger and I won't be pressured into marriage against—"

"Rutger?" Edward's disapproval was apparent. "You are far too informal with this man! Enough of this! We each have a duty to each other and to our family. If I could take care of you I would, but all I can do is arrange for someone else to do so in my stead."

"I see," quiet descended over them both. "Take care of me. Protect me. Arrange things for me. This is your duty?"

"As your brother, of course it is." Edward sounded puzzled.

"As I was going through your things for the basket, I found your ring."

"Yes, that's fine, but what does this have to do with—"

"You deliberately left it behind before you went to that meeting." It was Claire's voice that began to become unsteady. "Because you knew what you were doing was dangerous. You knew that you were putting yourself in jeopardy."

"It was my choice. I have to follow my own heart." He was defensive, his voice dropping.

"And my heart? Why won't you allow me a chance to follow mine?" She shot back.

"Because you're a woman, Claire. You have to be practical. You've already risked too much leaving England alone. Grayson has confused you and you've forgotten the rules that apply. But if it's love that you want, Lord Forthglade has told me he worships you. He can provide you security and marriage. He has no intention of smothering your spirit."

"I have no intentions of being smothered," she countered even as her own fears echoed Edward's. "Why can't I just stay in Savannah with you? I will petition for your freedom, or at the very least your comfort. Why do I have to marry anyone?"

He stood with the force of his emotions and lifted her by her arms, his frustrated grip bruising her arms. "Because it isn't safe here! Because if your identity is questioned, then all is lost! Because I can't survive this without knowing that you are being cared for! Damn it, Claire," he pulled her roughly into an embrace, "obey me, just this once. If you would just stop fighting me for one minute, you would see how right this is."

"I don't want to fight you," tears threatened as she held him possibly for the last time. "I would do anything to make you happy, but—"

"Then marry well. Accept Lord Forthglade's proposal and give me the strength I need to live through my sentence."

Claire pulled away from him, searching for an answer that would satisfy him without sacrificing her heart and soul. She had given herself to Rutger, but was more confused than ever about his true feelings and identity. She

Blind Aphrodite

loved him beyond reason, but that was the source of her fears. Beyond reason was a frightening place with no one to turn to, except Rutger. With her new understanding of all that marriage encompassed, the thought of another man's touch was revolting, even a kind man's such as Philip. She was in love with Rutger who was probably sailing from port while she stood here debating the lies she should tell her dearest twin brother. Samson had made it clear that there was no place for her on the *RavenSong* or in Rutger's life. At last, a profound sadness enveloped her as she realized that the last of her choices had likely sailed with the first high tide.

"As you wish, 'John'," she tried to turn away from him, but he caught her in his grip once again.

"Swear it, Claire," he urged her quietly, even as the sound of jangling keys came up the hallway. "Swear it and I'll be content."

"Be content then," she replied her face solemn with the impossible vow. "I will do as my duty compels me." He embraced her again with relief, and Claire shut her eyes against the darkness that never lifted, only to discover its cold grip on her heart.

"There now, mistress," the jailer's gruff voice interrupted their last embrace. "Time's up!"

"A few minutes more, please!" Edward pleaded, unwilling to end their last conference on such a dire note.

"Not for traitors, Mr. Bunting! Now step aside or you'll feel the lash!" The bulldog of a jailer bared his teeth, and Edward knew his threats were more than empty words.

"Oh, no!" Claire was alarmed, the harsh reality of Edward's existence pressing against her. "Please don't strike him!"

"Come now, miss," the jailer began to escort her from the room. "Let's not have a fuss."

Before she could protest or offer any last words to Edward, she found herself led down the hallway and back out into the jail's entrance. Tears spilled down her cheeks as she realized that she hadn't said good-bye. For the second time in one morning, she found herself walking away from someone she loved without a chance to say goodbye.

"Shall I call a carriage for you, miss?" the jailer offered, some of his gruffness lost in the face of genuine female distress.

"That won't be necessary, sir," Philip's voice startled them both from the doorway. "I will escort the lady, if she would allow me the honor."

Claire had trouble answering him past the tears and the lump in her throat, so she managed to at least nod miserably as a sign of agreement and reluctantly accepted his arm. His own carriage was waiting outside, and he gently assisted her into its comfortable compartment without any awkward directions. It reminded her of Rutger, and her tears began afresh.

"Here is my handkerchief, Miss Aylesbury," Philip offered quickly once he settled in across from her. "You have every right to cry, considering the circumstances."

She took the handkerchief gratefully as the horses pulled into the street and averted her face to try and recover her composure. She knew that Philip would attribute her tears to her parting with Edward alone and had no desire to enlighten him about the additional source of her pain. She ached to hear Rutger's voice, to be held in his arms again. She had sworn to obey Edward and accept Philip's offer, but a part of her still awaited one last rescue from her knight-errant.

Finally, she lifted her chin and made her best effort at appearing brave. "You have been all that is kind, Lord Forthglade."

"Not at all! I'm just glad I happened by." His voice was warm and friendly. "Now, I insist on taking you to supper."

"Oh, no," Claire's stomach lurched at the thought of a meal, her nerves still wrestling with her future. "I couldn't possibly—"

"Miss Aylesbury, I know that this has been a difficult parting and I just can't leave you alone with your grief. Forgive me, but it seems that you may need someone to talk to right now. Even if you aren't hungry."

Blind Aphrodite

Claire needed desperately to talk to someone, but her heart protested against this new confidante. Unable to think of a polite way to decline his offer, she nodded acceptance and forced a smile to her lips. "I'm not sure if I will be good company for you, Lord Forthglade, but perhaps you are right."

"It's settled then," he sounded pleased, and Claire leaned back and tried to think of anything but the price of her promises to Edward and the surrender of her dreams. Philip must have sensed her withdrawal, for he remained quiet for the remainder of the ride though the city streets. At last the carriage drew to a stop and Philip helped her alight.

"Where are we?" she asked as she took his arm for guidance.

"The Lion's Gate Inn. They have excellent fare and service. Would you prefer a private dining room or the hall?" He paid the driver as he spoke and then waited expectantly for her choice.

"The hall, please." She had not expected to find herself at the inn where he was staying and Claire's throat constricted at the thought of being alone with Philip, despite his outward show of gentlemanly consideration. She tried to dismiss her misgivings and reminded herself that Philip may very well be her husband before long. Still, a flutter of uneasiness remained as they entered the busy common room. Claire could hear the patrons engaged in lively conversation and the smell from the kitchen was tempting.

Philip led her to a cool and quiet corner and settled her in before summoning a waitress. He ordered a simple meal and wine, giving her time to relax in these new surroundings.

"Wine? Perhaps I shouldn't—" Claire began anxiously.

"It's early, I realize. But you look a little pale, and one glass won't hurt, I promise."

Her brow furrowed skeptically, but then she found herself smiling as he went on.

"Unless you're one of those ladies who overindulges and cannot stop at one glass! I can't imagine it, but if you're afraid of hopelessly embarrassing yourself or doing damage, I will at least swear to keep you from trying archery, hunting and all things dangerous."

"I'll have you know I was once a wicked archer, and I'm convinced I could still hit a ringing bell at twenty paces," Claire pulled up her shoulders in mock pride enjoying his teasing manner. "I suppose one glass wouldn't lessen my skills."

"Well," he sounded as if he were seriously considering, "I suppose *one* glass would be all right. But we may have trouble convincing someone to put an apple on their head and ring a bell later if they knew you'd been drinking."

"You won't volunteer, Lord Forthglade?" she asked innocently.

It was his turn to laugh. "I promised to be honest with you, so I'm afraid I would have to decline. Not that I doubt your skills! But you barely know me and what if you decide at the last that you'd rather put me out of my misery than tell me you won't marry me."

Some of her light mood fell at his mention of the proposal, and Claire wasn't sure how to respond.

"Oh, my!" Philip's tone was soothing. "Now I've done it! Here you were hoping to break my heart, and I've spoiled the surprise."

"Please don't say such things." Claire reacted quietly. "I have no hope of hurting anyone."

"Of course not, Miss Aylesbury," he tone was even and sincere. "I didn't mean to make you uncomfortable. Please remember what I said when I met you last. If you think of me as an ally, I would be most flattered."

The wine arrived and Philip filled two glasses while she considered his words.

"You were very encouraging to me, and I shouldn't have forgotten it. You're the only one urging me to follow my own instincts, and I'm grateful to you for that."

"Ah! Gratitude!" he sounded jovial again. "Come let's make a toast to gratitude!"

Blind Aphrodite

Claire reached out to find her glass to make the toast, only to feel it slip from her grasp and spill across the table. The commotion was sudden as Philip moved to avoid the liquid, the table seemed to shake and then Claire heard him gasp.

"Oh, dear!" Philip gave a shaky laugh. "You missed me entirely, but somehow I've managed to spill my own glass all over my coat!"

Claire blushed furiously convinced that he was only being polite. "I am so sorry, Lord Forthglade."

"Not at all!" he offered gentle reassurance. "I bumped the table and foiled myself, I swear!" He cleared his throat before continuing, "I am greatly embarrassed to ask, but would you mind allowing me to exchange coats. My room is upstairs and it shouldn't take but a moment."

"Of course." Claire fought the urge to apologize endlessly. She hated appearing like a fumbling helpless person in public, even while her common sense told her that sighted people spilled their drinks all the time.

"I don't wish to leave you alone in a public room, Miss Aylesbury. Can you accompany me upstairs?" He noticed her shocked hesitation and went on, "I would leave the door open, naturally."

"Oh," Claire knew she must seem like a ninny after he had treated her with only the greatest respect. The flutter of anxiety returned, but Claire was determined to prove to Lord Forthglade that she was as independent as he credited her to be. "Naturally, open will be fine." She took his hand and he led her up the stairs towards his rooms, unaware of the eyes that followed their progress.

Chapter Twenty-three

His interview with the prison ship's commander had been extremely fruitful, and Rutger had a better grasp of why his first bribe had yielded such quick results. Corrupt men rarely kept their secrets when offered better pay. Sir Brewster had apparently left payment with the commander right before their arrival in port to allow his cousin and a certain lady access to 'John Bunting' if requested. The 'certain lady' had turned out to be extremely beautiful, stopping in regularly with additional payments. Rutger's coins had provided a simple bonus. The commander had even admitted that the charges against John were practically meaningless, but if a man enjoyed the finer things in life he didn't question the orders of his superiors. Basil had been behind Claire's trouble almost from the beginning, along with Basil's mysterious 'cousin'. Rutger contained his rage and quickly made arrangements for John Bunting's death certificate.

The jail was his next stop, and Rutger braced himself for his second meeting with Edward. In light of their first encounter, he knew it was unlikely that this one would go much better. An image of Claire standing against the railing of the main deck of the *RavenSong* framed by the sunset, Claire looking at him with total trust, came into his mind. For Claire, he would see it through.

The jailer eyed him suspiciously, but after reviewing the sealed orders Rutger carried, became more cooperative. With a sigh, the jailer led Rutger through the solid iron door and down the corridor of cells to find

Blind Aphrodite

Edward. Since their last meeting, Edward's appearance had dramatically improved. A change of clothes, a chance to bathe and fresher air had restored him, and Rutger tried not to see how much of Claire looked back at him from behind Edward's blue-green eyes. As the door was unlocked, Edward stood with a cold glare at his unexpected visitor.

"All the time you need, governor," the jailer offered before leaving them alone.

Edward's was openly astonished. "All the time you need? However did you manage that, Grayson?"

Rutger shrugged his shoulders, "Unimportant. Is it true she's agreed to marry Philip?" He had intended to be direct, but Rutger almost winced at the question.

If Edward was taken aback, he didn't show it. "Yes, although it's no concern of yours."

"No, of course not." Rutger took a deep breath to steady his voice. "However I am curious to know what he offers in return for your consent."

"He has offered to take care of her, to secure her future and to continue to help me while I'm incarcerated." Edward's chin gave a signature lift that reminded Rutger of Claire, and Rutger tried not to smile.

"How was Lord Forthglade going to do that?" he pressed, "How was he helping you?"

"He arranged for me to see Claire, didn't he? And sent a physician! He has even arranged for better quarters on the *Laconia*." Edward's confidence faltered at the mention of the nightmare that awaited him aboard the prison ship. "But again, I don't see that this is any concern of yours, Grayson."

"I have a proposition for you, sir," Rutger moved further into the cell and lowered his voice to avoid being overheard. "One which I'm sure you'll find agreeable."

Edward's eyes narrowed warily. "A proposition?"

"It's simple, really," Rutger continued undaunted. "I arrange for your freedom and you leave immediately with Claire to return safely to England. In return, there will be no marriage to Lord Forthglade."

"What?" His shock was palpable.

"You heard me. She doesn't need 'protection'. She needs her brother, and once you're free there is little need to marry lying fortune hunters like Forthglade."

"Lying fortune hunters? I suppose you're suggesting that you are a better candidate?"

Rutger fought the urge to strike out and barely managed it. "I'm suggesting nothing of the kind. You're an idiot, Bunting. This is like arguing with a half-wit. *I'm* the one who arranged for your temporary release from the ship. *I'm* the one who sent Cutter, although that was my mistake to tell him to keep it anonymous. I had no idea you would credit Forthglade. And now *I'm* the one who is offering to buy your freedom. Take it or leave it, John."

"Why should I trust you?" Edward looked unconvinced, unsure of a benevolent offer from a man calling him an idiot and a half-wit.

"Why should you trust Forthglade? Impressed with his title? Or is it just his looks?" The question dripped with acid, and Rutger hated the echo of sarcasm that bounced off the stone walls. Worse, Edward's gaze dropped guiltily to the floor and Rutger knew there was a painful truth in it. "I thought so. Do you judge everyone by his or her appearance, Mr. Bunting? Willing to bet your life on that judgement?"

Edward's averted gaze shot up to Rutger's face and held as if Edward were trying to discern the truth behind the disturbing scars, "You'll arrange for my freedom. Why?"

"For Claire's sake," Anger fell away at the simple statement, and Rutger began to silently pray.

"For Claire's sake," Edward echoed the words with a whisper.

Blind Aphrodite

"Take her home where she belongs, John. Do it quickly. Or our ruse will be discovered and then there isn't enough gold to keep us both from ruin and the hangman's rope. Agreed?"

Time stood still as Edward's eyes locked with his. At last, reason prevailed. "Agreed."

"I've arranged passage aboard a sailing ship that leaves on tonight's high tide. Take what you want from your cell and hurry to find Claire at the Garden Street Inn." Rutger moved back to the iron bars. "Jailer!"

"How is this possible?" Edward was already grabbing a basket and shoving in his meager possessions.

"Prison fever. John Bunting died this morning from a fever. Justice is served and now you'll disappear so that no one can prove differently. It's contagious, so the jail and prison ship will be quarantined for a time to keep prying eyes from looking too closely at a singular death." Rutger's smile was humorless.

"Then you've already made the arrangements." Edward finished his packing and moved towards the door. "What would you have done if I hadn't agreed to your terms, Grayson?"

Rutger's smile didn't change, and he offered no response to the impossible question. Edward shivered a little at the uncompromising expression in the captain's golden eyes. For Claire's sake, Edward had no doubt that Grayson would have walked away without looking back leaving him to die.

The jailer arrived at the door and unlocked the padlock with a wry look at his now 'deceased' prisoner. "Step lively, man."

"After you, sir," Rutger bowed graciously and Edward needed no other prodding to move through the open door into the corridor. The dignity that had impressed Rutger aboard the *Laconia* returned, and Edward made his way on visibly shaking legs at a deliberate and leisurely pace as if he had been told that dinner was now being served in the salon.

At the entrance to the jail, he turned one last time to his benefactor. "I'm not sure how to thank you, sir. Claire will be—"

"There is no need to tell her of my involvement." Rutger's tone left no room for argument and Edward conceded the point quickly.

"As you wish, Grayson." Edward gave him a slight bow, and then left to find Claire and tell her the good news at his change in fortune.

Rutger waited a moment, gathering the storm of his thoughts set off by his final efforts to secure Claire's happiness. "At least she will be safe," he spoke aloud without realizing it.

"Course, your man will have to wait for her to get back to the inn with her fancy man." The jailer interjected, as if the conversation had included him all along.

"What?" Rutger wheeled around, fine-tuned instincts making him instantly alert. "What fancy man?"

"Brewster's cousin, Forthglade." The jailer grunted as if this information were too obvious to warrant discussion. "Surprised you didn't run into 'em as often as they come to see your boy the last couple of days."

"Claire is with Forthglade now?" Rutger was having trouble controlling his fear as a final horrible piece of the puzzle fell into place. The mysterious cousin was Forthglade, which meant that the villain had known where Edward was from the start.

"He came to pick her up after seeing the 'dead' bloke. I confess, I'll miss the rounder since all you gentlemen seem to pay so handsomely just to out-do each other for the little lady. Not that she didn't look to be worth the effort."

"How long ago did they leave?" Rutger's thoughts were racing.

"Couldn't say, could I?" The bulldog expression came over the man's squat face and Rutger shoved through the jail's open doors with impatient force. Damn! He might already be too late.

Chapter Twenty-four

⚭

"Here you are, Miss Aylesbury." Claire sat down on the soft cushions of the settee, wondering again at Philip's consistent attentiveness and sweet manners. "I'll be only a moment to find a better coat. I'm afraid in my current pungent attire, you won't need a bell to hit me from twenty paces."

Claire listened as he busied himself in the dressing room, and out of habit took inventory of the room. It felt larger than her rooms at the Garden, but lacked the large windows to give it greater light and fresh air. The room had a distinctly masculine odor, except for—except for the cloying scent of expensive perfume. Olivia's expensive perfume, a dry voice whispered in her head and the truth settled slowly as additional smells began to emerge. Underneath the sweet fragrance ran darker threads of musk and sweat—a scent that her recent night's experience made all too familiar. It was the smell of passion that hung in the air.

She stood with her heart pounding wishing only to be away from the room.

"What is it, Miss Aylesbury? Are you uncomfortable?" the voice was friendly, and Claire wondered how such deceit was possible.

"I wish to leave," Claire tried to keep her voice from trembling, as she began using her cane to edge towards the door. "I really am not the best company for you, I'm afraid."

"Nonsense. You are the very best company a man could wish for, my dear." His voice came from a direction she had not expected and the sound of the door shutting made her legs grow numb from terror.

"I am not your dear, Lord Forthglade." Claire hoped she sounded calm and regal. "I have decided to take your wisdom to heart. I can do what I wish, and I have no wish to remain here." She began to navigate towards the door more purposefully when a hand closed on her arm to prevent her.

"And where will you go? Not planning on returning to Captain Muck's arms, are we?" Sincerity melted away to caustic wit as Philip held her fast. "While you make quite a charming couple, I'm sure that's not what your brother had in mind when he ordered you to marry well."

Claire was speechless at the change in him, but recovered to try to brazen it out. "It is none of your concern, my Lord. Olivia has led you to presume a great deal, and for that I am sorry. As for Captain Grayson, he is expecting me any moment."

"Ah, Claire," his voice was almost sympathetic. "You haven't even begun to properly apologize for all the trouble you've caused. I haven't come all this way and spent all this time and effort to lose the prize now."

"Prize?" she barely managed a whisper as the horror beside her kept talking.

"Consider it a term of endearment, sweetest." Philip's grip began to tighten until she whimpered at the agony of his fingers digging into her arm. "I suggest you return to your seat so that we can talk about our future." He dragged her back to the settee, and sat next to her as if it were an ordinary occurrence to hold someone against their will.

"We have no future, Philip."

"Don't be ridiculous. Our future is already well underway." He sounded supremely confident and Claire's blood began to run cold. "London society believes that we have eloped. I had to work quickly to cover your little escapade. Your uncle is dead, thanks of course to the 'medicine' that Olivia provided. There's no time to waste."

Blind Aphrodite

"My uncle is dead?" It was unbelievable to Claire that her uncle, a man who had always seemed as strong as an ancient Norman fortress, should fall to treachery. "Why would you confess all this? What makes you think I won't go to the authorities?"

"It is Olivia that has poisoned him. There is no evidence that links me to the crime, and as your husband, I'm afraid I won't be allowing you to go anywhere without my permission."

"You are *not* my husband!" she tried to stand, but he pulled her back with a vicious yank.

"Pardon me, you're right." His politeness was chilling. "Fiancée would be more accurate, but as I see it, legally that makes you my wife in all but practice."

"You're insane!" Panic began to set in and Claire knew that if it overtook her she would be lost. "You and Olivia both in some bizarre scheme to work everything to your advantage. Well, threaten all you wish! Blind, deaf and dumb, I wouldn't marry you!"

"In love with someone else, my dear?" he asked quietly. "I warn you, you're giving me a headache."

"What?" His odd comment about a headache convinced her that he was completely mad.

"In love with the captain, I know." He released her arm and moved away from the small couch to pace the room. Claire realized it was actually worse to have him stalking about the room and her terror grew with every word. "Strange, isn't it? He fancies himself in love with you, the poor, desperate man. He said you had the clearest vision of anyone he had ever met and that he was convinced it was the rest of the world that is blind. Of course, when I explained to him that it was your clarity of vision that had led you to agree to become my wife and vow eternal love—he didn't seem to have a clever response."

"Rutger," she whispered his name, a nightmare image of Philip's poisonous lies making him believe that she loved anyone but him.

Suddenly Philip was in front of her and lifting her from the couch to face him. "You're forgetting Edward, my dear."

"No!" The coil of fear drew tighter when she realized he was right. She had forgotten her twin.

"It was my dear cousin Basil who unwittingly was able to arrange for his capture. And now his life rests entirely in my hands. You marry me, or Edward dies. It is as simple as that." His voice changed as he drew her closer. "I confess, I think you will make an ideal wife, Claire."

"No," she was almost paralyzed by his threats and the unreality of the situation.

"Your face is so expressive. I am sure I will never grow tired of watching that delicious play of fear in your eyes. They say that when you lose one of your senses, the others become keener. Shall we experiment with that, Claire?"

She began to scream until he covered her mouth with one of his hands and pushed up against the wall. He was stronger than she had first realized but when his free hand began to claw at the front of her dress, anger and fear made her fight like a wild animal. His hand slipped and she sank her teeth into his palm gagging against the coppery taste of his blood in her mouth. He drew back with a cry, and then the world seemed to explode in constellations of sickening pain as he slapped her with all his force. The imprint of his hand blazed across her cheek and Claire began to whimper at the cold gray mist that edged into the dark field of her vision.

"Oh, yes," he purred against her throat as the cloth of her dress yielded to his force and her breasts were bared to his touch. "So sweet and firm— it will be worth a year of bucking that practiced whore Olivia to finally have you, my dear."

Claire writhed to escape him, sobbing at the weakness that crept into her limbs when there was a terrible blast of musket fire and Philip's weight suddenly shifted away. Relief and shame swept through her and Claire

Blind Aphrodite

wished the room would stop spinning so that she could thank her savior. She clutched at the torn remnants of her neckline and called out "Rutger?"

"T-Tigress?" Philip's voice sounded hollow as he turned towards the intruder. "You...you forget the game, dearest."

"I forget nothing, Philip." The icy tone made Claire cringe in shock as she realized it was Olivia. "I forget *nothing!*" Another shot rang out with the sound of wood splintering.

"Olivia," Philip staggered towards his mistress, "My head hurts." His speech was thick and began slurring as he continued. "Come un' pay your debts, tigreth. Come un' pay."

A groan escaped his lips and Claire held her breath at the sound of his body falling to the floor.

"I killed him! I killed him!" Olivia's screams were demonic howls and then suddenly Claire was knocked down and Olivia's hands were around her neck with a deadly hold. "I killed him for you, Claire! All for you"

Claire's hands were slick with sweat and blood and she couldn't seem to get a purchase on Olivia's fingers. The nightmare had no end as she struggled for air.

"I loved him, Claire! All for you!" Olivia hissed in her ear as Claire felt a strange heaviness spread through her. Gray united with black, and for one glorious moment Claire was sure that every color of the rainbow flooded into her eyes before the darkness overcame it and there was nothing.

*   *   *

Rutger had believed that he would never again see anything as horrifying as he had that fateful day on the *RavenSong's* gun deck. The sight of Olivia strangling a limp and apparently lifeless Claire in a pool of Philip's blood made him rethink what hell might have in store for the damned. He leapt across the room to pull Olivia from Claire, ignoring Edward's cry behind him, as he stood stunned in the doorway trying to understand what his eyes conveyed.

"Olivia?" Edward began to stumble forward, shock making him clumsy.

"Hold her, Edward." Rutger had eyes only for Claire, as he shoved a babbling Olivia towards Edward. "Claire! Oh, no," he surveyed her quickly, the bruises on her neck against her pale skin. He laid a hand against her cool cheek and forced himself to lay his ear to her chest, desperate for any sign.

"All for you! I killed them both for you, darling! Would you like to have a taste then, my lord?" Edward tried to keep a hold of his charge while watching desperately as his sister lay unmoving. Olivia's last question was accompanied by a kiss, and Edward pushed away in disgust as she shoved her tongue into his mouth and groped between his legs.

"Keep her quiet, damn it!" Rutger roared in frustration. "I can't hear!"

"I killed them both!" Olivia began screaming, and the innkeeper and several patrons from downstairs began to tumble into the room to marvel at the scene.

"I killed them both!" her screams became sobs, and Rutger gave up his fruitless efforts only to draw his beloved Claire into his arms to rock her soundlessly back and forth. The rest of the room disappeared as he caressed her hair and began to whisper meaningless comfort into her ears. In a fog, he heard someone scream for the constable but his world consisted of the soft and slight weight in his arms. He couldn't think past his loss, or see beyond the glassy wall of agony that separated him from her. "Safe now, my Lady Claire. You're safe now."

A still screaming Olivia was being held by the landlord and two patrons, freeing Edward to at last reach Claire. Edward knelt next to Rutger, grieving openly at the sight of his beautiful sister in the arms of her captain. Rutger's face was turned so that his left cheek was buried in

Blind Aphrodite

her hair, and Edward's heart broke at how perfectly matched they now seemed. "Please let me take her."

Rutger glared at him, only to begin to woodenly release her into her brother's waiting arms. Claire's soft whimper made him freeze as her fingers gripped his waistcoat in protest. "Oh god, Claire!" He could feel the growing heat of her against his chest, and began to rock her again, as she lay unmoving but miraculously alive in his arms. "Safe now, my Lady Claire."

"She's alive!" Edward exclaimed with tears of joy, only to hear Olivia's screams renew.

"No! I killed her! She deserves to die, don't you see? I am Lady Forthglade! Kill her!" Olivia's struggles ceased, as she seemed to faint against the hands that held her fast.

"The constable and officer of the watch should be here any minute, gentlemen. Is the lady all right?" the innkeeper asked from the doorway, distraught at the disturbance in his normally quiet establishment.

Rutger felt cold logic return as he surveyed the chaos of the room. Philip's now clouded eyes stared up mockingly from the floor at Rutger's dilemma. Lord Forthglade's hawk-like features had twisted on one side as if to parody his nemesis. Even in death, Rutger had a sense that Philip's evil might still harm them. Rutger had to get Edward and Claire clear of the room before the authorities arrived. With Edward so newly 'reborn' as himself, it was critical to have him safely away before too many questions were asked about the Earl of Clarence' whereabouts in the last few months.

"Take her back to the Garden and do everything you can to bring her safely away from this." Rutger wasted no time waiting for Edward's protests as he gently placed Claire into her brother's arms. "Go!" 'I'll remain and explain everything to the authorities," he spoke quietly and then stood to speak more loudly for the rest of the room to hear. "She requires medical attention. My carriage is waiting and I'll tell the constable where she is so that he can interview her later."

"But how will you—" Edward began to ask only to find himself 'helped' from the room by Claire's grim champion.

"Make way, gentleman. She needs air. Go!" The crowd cooperated instantly, clucking their concern for the handsome twins and some offering their advice for her care or which doctor Edward should summon. As soon as he was sure that Edward had been allowed to leave with Claire, he turned his attention back to the crime. Rutger turned to lift Olivia from the floor to lay her across the bed.

"Should we send for a doctor for her as well, sir?" the landlord tentatively offered.

His first reaction was to say no, but as he looked down on Olivia, he considered that a lack of mercy might have been the cause of her illness in the first place. "As you will, sir."

The constable arrived and Rutger was amused at the relief on everyone's faces, as if the problem would be magically resolved, the dead restored and justice done. He had less cause to be optimistic, as the constable began his questions and cursory investigation. Fortunately, several witnesses were able to collaborate his version of events. They all told of hearing musket fire and a woman screaming "I killed him," before Rutger and Edward ran into the room. They identified Olivia as a confessed murderer, and the constable's discovery of a woman's clothes in the room's wardrobe confirmed her fate as a jealous lover. Lord Forthglade had been indiscreet and made inappropriate advances to Miss Aylesbury, setting off the tragic chain of events. Rutger's place in the story seemed less clear.

"I am a friend of the family," he offered without any additional explanation.

"And how was it that you happened upon the scene to rescue Miss Aylesbury?" the constable prodded.

"My good fortune, I suppose."

"Your name, sir?" he asked gruffly.

Blind Aphrodite

"Grayson." He bowed stiffly, hating the way the man stared at his face. "Why is that name familiar to me?"

"I cannot imagine, sir, since I only just arrived in Savannah two weeks ago."

"A new regular at the Red Wolf Tavern, sir?" his gaze was unshakable.

Rutger felt himself stop still at the unexpected question. "Yes, I suppose."

The constable nodded at this, and ordered his deputies to carry the accused murderess to the jail to be held for trial. "As for you sir, please come with me to meet the magistrate. I believe he would like to question you about another matter entirely."

"As you wish, sir." Rutger picked up his hat where it had fallen, giving one last glance towards Philip's stiffening face. The mocking grimace mirrored his own and Rutger wondered if he were about to sacrifice more than his freedom by the end of the day.

Chapter Twenty-five

In the dream, her throat was on fire but as she turned away from a gentle pressure on her forehead, the bruises on her neck made her all too aware that she was awake. Claire opened her eyes and tried to understand where she could be—only to hear a familiar voice make her wonder if she might still be asleep.

"Claire? Are you awake, dearest?" his tone was the embodiment of anxiety.

"Edward?" she croaked, wincing at the pain speech caused her. "Am I in prison?"

"Shhh," he soothed instantly pressing a cold cloth against her temples. "You're safe at the Garden Street Inn. I would say, safe and sound, but I'm afraid that would be exaggerating."

"Edward!" she struggled to try to sit up only to have Edward gently hold her back. "What are you doing here? Did you escape? Where is Rutger—Captain Grayson?"

"Calm yourself, Claire," he smiled to see the familiar spirit in her questions. "I've been released—in a manner of speaking. 'John Bunting' has been recorded as lost to a fever, and a bribe allowed me to leave just like a ghost." He embraced her.

"Oh, Edward," she whispered, "I'm so happy!"

"We'll need to leave Savannah tonight if possible, since even ghosts can be questioned. You can recover aboard ship and then we're safe in England where I can take care of you."

Blind Aphrodite

She could hear the beaming smile in his voice, but suddenly her memory returned and the burning in her throat made her sit up quickly, eluding Edward's well meant restraints. "Philip! What happened to Lord Forthglade?"

"Don't think about him, Claire. He's dead. Olivia killed him and then attacked you." His voice was serious in the quiet of the room. "I can't tell you how awful I feel knowing that I actually pressed you to marry the scoundrel. He seemed like the answer to all my problems, and I trusted Olivia completely. How could I have been so wrong?" He began to pace to try to keep up with his thoughts. "When Forthglade warned me about Grayson, I saw no reason to doubt him. But why would Grayson have brought you to Savannah if his intentions were dishonorable? Why make any effort to find me at all? Why arrange for my freedom?"

"We were all fooled by Philip and Olivia," she offered what comfort she could, still amazed at the web of lies that had come so close to destroying their lives. "Sir Brewster is his cousin and arranged for your capture at Lord Forthglade's direction. It was all a huge plot to attain our fortunes. They used our love for each other against us, Edward." She paused for only a moment, "How long have I been unconscious? Where *is* Captain Grayson?"

"Only a couple of hours. As for Grayson, it doesn't matter." His evasiveness frightened her.

"Is he all right? Is he still in port?" a new urgency crept into her ragged voice.

"Grayson is fine! He's dealing with the authorities until you and I are safely away. It's over now," she felt him straighten his shoulders with his resolve. "We shall put our fortunes in order, and you shall be free to do whatever you wish, I swear it."

"Edward!" Claire was astonished at the change in him.

"I will keep the wolves at bay, and you shall have the best care in the world once we return to England."

"No!" she pushed away from him, fighting a wave of gray dots at the sudden movement.

"Claire! You're upsetting yourself!"

"I am not upsetting myself." She took a deep breath and tried to ignore the pain, as she stood to put on her dressing gown. "I love you, as only a twin sister can. But you are not going to become my keeper. I am not some blind animal that needs special treatment. Go home to England if that is your desire. But I realize that I don't want anyone to shield me. I know what I want and don't need your permission to seek my own happiness."

"Claire—" he began only to be stopped by the undeniable light in her eyes.

"I have to follow my own heart, Edward." She waited for the arguments and countless reasons why she was being stubborn or hysterical, only to be folded once more into his brotherly embrace.

"I suppose it's your turn, Claire. How can I love you and even consider stopping you?" he laughed until the ache in his chest lessened at the thought of losing her so soon, but the image of Grayson rocking her in his arms made it easier. "I'll stay in Savannah until you're sure—"

"I'm sure, Edward," she smiled at the habitual worry. "I'm not an invalid or a child. Now, if you don't mind I want to get dressed now. I must see Rutger."

"Rutger, is it?" he asked gruffly, making one last attempt at being the protective older brother.

"You may wait downstairs and summon a carriage for me as soon as I'm ready." She dismissed him with a smile, and Edward left to carry out her orders.

"As you wish, madam," he teased her from the doorway, "Anything else?"

"Thank you, Edward."

Blind Aphrodite

"Good luck, Claire." He closed the door behind him, and Claire crossed to her wardrobe and rang for Bess. Her hand found the ivory dress she had first worn when she had made her 'great escape' and she prayed for one last chance for adventure.

Chapter Twenty-six

Olivia's screams through the walls were unnerving in the confines of the magistrate's office and the small man winced at the irrational cries. He sighed and forced his attention back to the remarkable man that sat across from his table for questioning.

"What is this regarding, sir?" Rutger's own patience was wearing thin, aware that his own fears and personal knowledge of his less than legal past activities were adding to the room's tension.

"One of the wenches at the Red Wolf tavern was murdered recently."

"Which one?" Rutger leaned forward intently hoping for a name unknown to him.

"A girl named Merry. One of the other girls mentioned that she had had a couple of regular gentlemen callers in the last two weeks. Both newcomers."

Rutger's shock was genuine, and he closed his eyes at a growing sense of dread. "And you suspect me."

"Your name was noted by my officer as having recently gained her favors, but—"

"Do you have a description of the other 'newcomer'? Rutger asked quietly. "Did he have dark hair and hawk-like features?"

"Yes!" it was the magistrate's turn to lean forward intently. "Do you know him?"

Blind Aphrodite

"Philip Trent, Lord Forthglade. He is unfortunately your newest murder victim, sir. Miss Kent has apparently dispatched him on your behalf."

"How convenient for you," the judge responded wryly, only to wince as Olivia began screaming the word, 'whore' over and over.

"Magistrate, you and I both know that my face would be impossible to forget. I would be willing to bet one pound British sterling that you won't forget it for as long as you live. Do you honestly think I could have somehow slipped into the Red Wolf unnoticed last night?"

"You may have a point, sir."

"Do you have witnesses that say differently?" he pressed carefully.

"The wench said she never saw him except for a silhouette in the doorway. You could have kept to the shadows and accused this other man, knowing him to be beyond questions in the grave." The magistrate conjectured.

"And what would my motive be?" he asked striving to keep his tone even.

"Perhaps she rejected you for your looks, if I may be blunt, sir."

Rutger nodded at this, "Yet there are no doubt witness to countless offers that Merry made to me that would convey the opposite. It was I who rejected her advances."

"Really?" the magistrate's stern countenance dropped at his surprise.

"Thank you for the compliment, sir." Rutger tried not to let the man's reactions sting.

"I'm afraid this matter will take some investigation, and for now, you are my primary suspect. I will have you held here until we can prove—"

Olivia interrupted with a wicked laugh and then "Merry cries, Merry dies, Whore's that dance, don't stand a chance, Philip!"

Rutger seized his last chance at freedom, knowing that his monstrous appearance would only prejudice a jury against him. "It seems there may be another witness after all. She knows me, perhaps I can reach her so that she can tell us what she knows."

The magistrate seemed shaken by the last outburst, and slowly nodded agreement. "I must be present to witness your conversation. You cannot lead her. She is clearly unstable and so you will have to phrase your questions carefully."

"Agreed." Rutger stood and with the magistrate and two uniformed guards was led to Olivia's cell. The magistrate indicated that he should go forward without them, as they listened in the corridor. As he stood in the dim hallway, he realized that this desperate chance was more desperate than he'd considered. Olivia was huddled against the wall and when she saw him her face was disfigured with sheer loathing. He had just placed his life into the hands of an insane woman who hated him.

She unfolded from the small cot and approached the bars with all the prim grace he recalled from their first meeting. "Captain Ogre, have you come to beg?"

"What should I beg for, Olivia?" he kept his eyes on her face.

"For her life, of course." She snarled at him, and then as if remembering her manners gave him a stunning smile.

"For whose life?" he prayed the question wouldn't annoy her into meaningless screams.

"Everything I did was for Philip's pleasure, you know. I was to be Lady Forthglade! I am a gentlewoman, do you hear me?" To his horror, she began to cry. "He m-made me degrade myself. I g-g-gave my soul to the devil, and now I am Lady Forthglade."

"You are Lady Forthglade, Olivia." Rutger wasn't sure where the thread was leading, or how much patience the magistrate might have for her meaningless babble. "Did Philip's pleasure include hurting anyone else, Olivia?"

"You're a fool, Ogre. A man like my Philip has sophisticated tastes and his needs *must* be met. You could never be half the man he is."

"To be sure." He conceded easily, frightened by the haughty disconnected look in her eyes.

"Beg me, Ogre and I'll give you her life." At his hesitation, she screeched, "Beg me!"

Blind Aphrodite

Rutger knelt before the bars and tried not to think of the judge who watched just a few feet away as he prepared to grovel if his next gamble didn't succeed. "And what if I could give you Philip's life in return, Olivia?"

She knelt on the other side of the bars, her eyes feral in the dim light. "Do you think I'm beautiful, Ogre?"

"Yes, very much so."

"And you wouldn't need maids or wenches to satisfy your appetite would you? You wouldn't need them if I knew all their whore's tricks? I would be all you needed in a wife, yes?" He forced himself not to look away as she began to suggestively rub up against the bars.

"Like Philip?" he asked as his heart filled with dread.

"No!" she screamed and pushed away from the bars. "He never meant to touch them! It was for the sensation of it! That dark haired witch just made him forget his promises that's all!"

"And the wench at the Red Wolf?" he held his breath.

"She had to die, Ogre! She lied to us about you! He never wanted her! He came home and said he wanted only me! Only me! I am Lady Forthglade! They raped me while he watched and he wanted only me! Only me!" She began to laugh and cry at the same time, and Rutger backed away from the mortifying sight of it. Olivia began to howl like a wounded animal, and then stopped as if slapped.

"Captain Grayson?" she sounded bewildered and small, and his heart ached at the sight of her lost expression. Slowly, she reached up and unpinned the long golden braid of her hair. He watched mesmerized at the timeless gesture and the unconscious beauty of the picture she created in the midst of the jail's ugly gray stone and iron. The braid fell to below her knees, and the first inkling of dread began to form within him.

"Olivia?" he asked, his throat constricting with an unspoken fear. "Guards!"

She smiled at him, and then it happened even as the guards rushed forward to try to open the doors to stop it. She wound the braid around the high bar of the room's only tiny window and tied a knot. Then like some macabre ballet dancer leapt towards the small square of fading light only to let herself fall against the wall as her neck was snapped by her own beautiful hair.

Numb fingers finally managed to unhinge the padlock, but there was no one left to save by the time they reached her body. Rutger stayed in the corridor fighting his own demons as his mind replayed again and again her last smile.

"You are free to go, Mr. Grayson." The magistrate was as pale as snow, and Rutger was sure his color was similar.

"You'll have to forgive me if I don't seem grateful." Rutger took a deep breath. "She deserved better, sir." He made his way out without looking back. If ever he was unsure of the depths of Forthglade's depravity, he vowed to remember the look on Olivia's face before she took her own life.

Chapter Twenty-seven

Claire ran a careful hand along the post's intricate lines, comforted to find a familiar curled tail, tiny lizard claws and head amidst the leaves. The wait for Rutger's return had not been uneventful. Samson had bristled protectively at the sight of her, but it was Cutter who had intervened to finally convince him that it was for Muck alone to send her away if he chose to. She still wasn't used to Rutger's nickname, but on Cutter's lips it hadn't seemed so shocking. She even tried saying it aloud in his empty quarters as if to summon him by magic. She imagined him with her in the room and tried to say it with all the force of her love for him, "Muck."

"Claire."

His voice made her reel about, smiling at her undiscovered gift for magic. "You came!"

"Where else would I be going?" He tried to jest, but her unexpected presence on board made him feel wary. The lanterns were lit and the flames fluttered with the early evening breeze through the windows. She looked more angel than goddess in her ivory dress, and Rutger hoped he would remember her always frozen in this moment. He should have known that she wouldn't leave without first coming to tell him farewell.

"Rutger—" she began.

"Thank God, you seem recovered," he cut her off nervously, not sure if he was ready for this last meeting. "Hours ago, we feared the worst."

"So much has happened," she added as her thoughts trailed his. Claire wanted to rush across the room into his arms, but her own nerves held her back. Finally, she reached out her hand, and Rutger drew closer to take it. His fingers were strong and callused and Claire gathered courage from the heat of him. "Thank you for my life, and for Edward's."

"I did very little, Claire." He deflected her praise unable to say much more for fear of babbling like a brook at the sight of her beloved face lifted to his. "When I arrived to deliver the death certificate, the jailer mentioned that you had left with Philip. I only wish I could have gotten to you faster."

"How in the world did you manage to arrange for Edward's freedom?" she asked, her curiosity evident.

"You managed it actually," he explained simply. "I used the necklace. I should have thought of it the first day we realized where he was, but I wasn't thinking straight at the time. I seem to have spent far too much time worrying about losing you. I don't think I've ever dreaded a goodbye more my entire life."

"Are you going to say goodbye, Rutger?" Her heart filled her eyes and she heard him catch his breath before he answered.

"What else can I say? Lord Forthglade may have been evil incarnate, but he was right about one thing. He never mistook me for a hero with a noble cause. You were the only cause that I cared about." He dropped her hand and walked over to look out of the open window towards the lantern lights of a town he now loathed. "What advantage do I offer you? I am the youngest son of four brothers to a lesser nobleman. My ship is my fortune and my crew the only real family I have. To finally tip the scales in my favor, while fighting for profit for my own country's blockade, I managed to lose half of my face so that I look like the devil himself."

"I see." Claire tipped her head to one side as if considering his words. "Describe yourself then, Lucifer."

Blind Aphrodite

"Are you being cruel, Claire?" He looked back from the window amazed at her strange request.

"Not at all. Should I try to describe you then?" Rutger was speechless, and she decided his silence indicated consent. "Your hair is dark brown—"

"It's blonde." He corrected, determined to stop the game before it went any further.

"Your eyes are the color of the sky, a nice blue—" She began again undaunted.

"I think they're amber, Claire. This is pointless—"

"How lovely!" Her smile was radiant as her imagination began to paint a better picture of the man before her.

Rutger's heart lurched at the sight and he tried to interrupt. "Claire, I'm far from—"

"You seem handsome to me, Rutger! You are brave and honorable. You set everything aside to help me and to save Edward's life. You've done nothing but try to protect me. I see no devil here."

"What can I offer you so that I don't feel like a thief whenever you look at me?"

Claire's chin rose with defiance and her voice rang with determination. "You're right, of course! My list of demands is fairly long and I can be quite stubborn. I want a man who will stand beside me only because he wants to—and not for fortune or title. I want a man who won't treat me as if I'm blind, but lets me see into his heart. The world awaits, Captain, and I'll need someone who wants to show it to me. I want the advantage of a life full of experience. I want someone who is strong enough to love me beyond question. And most of all—" she took a shaky breath wondering if she had gone too far.

"And most of all?" he urged her with a playful growl.

"I want to be able to love you all the days of my life. What better advantage could a woman hope for?" Shyness flitted across her features, and she seemed to watch him hopefully for his reply.

Renee Bernard

He laughed with sheer joy as years of pain disintegrated at her glance. "I love you, Claire. You have the most unique way of looking at things." Rutger swept her into his arms and began to rain light tender kisses down on her face

She reached up to take his face into her bare hands with a smile. "I see only what is true, Rutger. Only what is true."

Epilogue

◯

1784

The ball was a glittering feast of color and movements, and Rutger was doing his best to make his descriptions of the scene amusing for his wife. Claire was glowing with pleasure at the attempt and giggled when he told her that Lady Van Cleeves looked like a walrus in a sunflower costume.

"Can you see Edward?" she asked, hoping to divert Rutger from his clever game. She loved his sense of humor, but feared that in this instance he might inadvertently get them both into trouble.

The cream of London society was in attendance and invitations for the gala had been zealously sought after. Lord Edward Aylesbury was host, but it was Sir Grayson and his beautiful bride that drew toast after toast. The popular tale of their romance combined with the glitter of her wealth and his dashing image as a scarred buccaneer made them irresistible as a couple.

"I'm afraid I can't make him out in this mob of—" Rutger stopped himself as the object of his search caught his eye. "There he is! Driving all the mothers wild by aloofly talking to a group of dusty businessmen and apparently refusing to dance with their milk-toast daughters." Rutger smiled and then leaned over to whisper conspiratorially, "A brilliant plan of his, I'm sure, to throw those cows off pace."

"Rutger!" she gasped in astonishment at his cheek.

Blind Aphrodite

"Speaking of brilliant plans," he added without apology, enjoying the delicate blush that colored her face, "I believe I have one of my own." And with that, he gently guided a now laughing Claire out a pair of ornate French doors and into a moonlit garden.

"You are incorrigible, Captain," she countered, grateful for the escape from the heated, overcrowded ballroom into the cool night air. The garden leaves rustled in a soft breeze, and Claire inhaled the fragrance of jasmine and roses. A flutter of nerves made her take an extra moment or two before asking the question that had plagued her recently. She loved him so completely that it frightened her to contemplate his displeasure. "Rutger?"

Her tone and tender expression caught his attention immediately, and he led her to a stone bench where they would be undisturbed. "What is it, Lady Claire?"

"Have you been happy?" Claire held her breath, sure of the answer but unsure of how to guide him to her great news.

"Of course!" Rutger sounded puzzled. "Deliriously happy. Why do you ask?"

Claire smiled, "Samson once told me that the *RavenSong* wasn't a 'floating pleasure barge', but after these last few years, I would be forced to disagree. It has been heavenly to travel the world, and even to return to London for brief seasons now and again. Because you've made it heavenly."

"I'm flattered to hear you say all this, but I sense you're trying to tell me something." He took both of her hands into his. "So stop scaring me and out with it."

"Would you miss it terribly, the *RavenSong*, if we stayed in England for a time?"

"In England? I thought you wanted to see the—"

She cut him off with a kiss and Rutger lost his train of thought. The magic of her touch and the shadowy garden captured his senses and awakened a passion that never seemed far from the surface with Claire at his side.

Time had done nothing to diminish the effect of her presence and instead had only increased his desire to be with her.

"I hate to interrupt this scene of matrimonial bliss," Edward teased and the lovers drew apart reluctantly. "But I'm afraid you're too noticeable a couple to be allowed to quietly slip from the room."

Rutger stood with a soft growl, restrained from anger by Claire's soft touch on his elbow. He had come to an awkward truce with his brother-in-law in the last four years, as Edward struggled to accept Rutger's place in her life. "I am going to take that as a supreme compliment, Lord Aylesbury."

"Honestly! Don't the two of you ever tire of this?" Claire's chiding was softened by a smile that conveyed only affection for the contrasting pair.

"Never!" Edward stepped forward to take her other arm. "Besides, Rutger enjoys it as much as I do. And now that I am about to become a loving uncle, it's my duty to make sure the next generation doesn't take him too seriously."

"Well, at least you're—" Rutger stopped as Edward's words were underlined by Claire's quiet reaction. A breeze caught her hair and pulled back the curls that had fallen across her cheek. She was suddenly still and solemn, her eyes turned to him filled with confirmation and hope. "Is this true, Claire?"

Claire wanted to thrash her brother for blurting out her news, but understood that Edward would have known just by looking at her. She only wished he were equally astute to realize that she hadn't yet had a chance to break the news to Rutger. Claire had only just discovered her condition and had waited for the right moment, fearful that Rutger would be disappointed to leave the *RavenSong* for a period of time. Or worse, that he wouldn't want to leave the ship at all and would leave her in England to be safe. "Edward, we will rejoin the party in a moment."

"Oh, of course, I'm—I'm sorry to have—" Edward looked appropriately embarrassed and left them to their conversation.

Blind Aphrodite

"Rutger," Claire took a deep breath and tried to ignore her fears. "I meant to tell you this evening, but I wasn't sure if you would be pleased. It would mean staying here for my confinement."

"My Lady Claire," Rutger pulled her into his arms, "It wouldn't be possible for a man to be more pleased!"

"But the *RavenSong* is your sanctuary!" Claire felt as if a great weight were beginning to fall from her shoulders.

"*You* are my sanctuary, Claire," Emotion made his voice deeper than usual. "I don't care where we are, so long as we're together. Surely, you know that." And then there were no words for the joy that he felt and he kissed away any doubts she may have had. He lifted her into his arms and swept her deeper into the shadows of the hedges even as his mouth traced the promise of a garden that would never fade against her skin.

Claire was breathless from the sensation of his kisses and being held weightless in his arms. She gave into her own desires with a small sigh, and decided there would be time enough later to tell him that Bess had predicted twins.

About the Author

Renee Bernard lives in the Sierra-Nevada foothills of Northern California with her husband and family (two dogs and a cat). She has been writing historical romance for several years and this is her first published work.